Λ ♦ R ♦ G ♦ V ♦ R ♦ Λ

One phrase from *Argura* – 'imploded strophe and dispersed canzone' – sets an internalized choral impulse alongside a diffuse songlike one, the 'dispersed canzone' still pledged to argument. This criss-cross defines a compositional zone which, though contemporary, does not grant automatic access: this finding may be the controlling one behind *Argura*.

Also by John Peck from Carcanet

Broken Blockhouse Wall
Poems and Translations of Hĭ-Lö

JOHN PECK

A·R·G·V·R·A

D.   M.

J͡HS   F͡MR

VITA MVTATVR NON TOLLITVR

and moves one seeing down a fated groove of mind
with urging restlessness that stirs forth the flame

CARCANET

First published in 1993 by
Carcanet Press Limited
208-212 Corn Exchange Buildings
Manchester M4 3BQ

A CIP catalogue record for this book
is available from the British Library.
ISBN 1 85754 008 5

The publisher acknowledges financial assistance
from the Arts Council of Great Britain.

Set in 10pt Palatino by Bryan Williamson, Frome
Printed and bound in England by SRP Ltd, Exeter

Some poems in this book have appeared in the following, to whose editors grateful acknowledgement is hereby made: *Agenda, Gradiva, Ironwood, The New Republic, Partisan Review, Ploughshares, PN Review, Salmagundi, Tri-Quarterly, Yale Review.* Several others first appeared in a Festschrift for Thom Gunn, *A Few Friends* (Stonyground Press) and in Mrs Elizabeth Henry's *The Vigour of Prophecy* (University of Bristol). Parts of the book were first drafted during a period of support from the John Simon Guggenheim Memorial Foundation.

"Kayak Island" includes a version of several lines from Saint Augustine's commentaries on the Psalms. "Riddle of Peace" incorporates a version of the anonymous medieval Irish "Inten bec".

My title corresponds to no single Latin word, but rather to elements that derive from roots shared among several terms. The epigraph interprets lines by Guido Cavalcanti.

The cover design is based on a mosaic fragment from S. Giovanni Evangelista, Ravenna, *c.* 6th century.

Contents

◆

Mastarna, ochre stride along one grave wall,
one ripple among purple stutters of Claudius,
with mist shearing over the mountain still
central, and the cries nestling up there,

Mastarna who would have lent a fine clang
to a children's ditty, who knows if you were worth saving?

Three schoolgirls march past the lifted barrier,
the crossing guard lights his pipe.

Sahara Frescoes, Tassili

These were not guilty. Care was blind care
without puff-drift from a gouged acre
or ozone burnt back through stratosphere –

neither x-ray nor photograph nor
decodable fantasy nor sheer
index of the fleetingness we bear,

but a common trace on the high wall
of passage, milk and rock powder's full
shimmering caravan in profile,

as surf ripples along the dune's break
to a bound wave pulsing from each stroke
of the inner fountain, man awake –

bull's hump, elephant's radar-web ear,
delicate furred dong of jackal, hair
hive on the bride backlit by dawn's roar:

for when ice rolled back and sun strengthened
over the great middle garden, wind
herded our tribe chanting, drove with sand

through jonquil and blood ochres crushed in
shoulder blades, and led across the green-
abandoned advancing wash of stone.

The Capital, 1980

Between the Archives and Justice
the high banshee lisp of the riptooth
but louder still through the carpenter's truck door
We doan wan no ed yu kay shun
into the unanchored slant
of unrenewed definition,
where Whitman learned to sit the hours
of terminal love with his wounded,
tempted in line of duty to play favorites,
and where on the outbound commuter
a man stood prating in the valor of drunkenness
about his colonel
                    "Don't worry", he says,
*"I've slated you for the one-tenth
who ain't going to 'Nam"*
                              the car wobbling him
as a bell clanged without reference to the stops
*When that kinda thing happens
it kinda makes you think...*
slack-jawed under the dinging
signal too rapid to be fateful
and too slow to sound a warning

Leaving the Central Station

   Now that my own was moving,
now that change was sliding in, quickening,
faces on the platform hinted things
striving to show themselves, to touch the fact
of weight unmooring into vague futures, blank –
but then I sat up and turned: *Haydn!* a sharp pull,
not the face but the fact of Haydn, that tug
part of the speed, colors beginning to run,
spreading out to take the name now, *Mozart!*
and it was no face in particular,
with sweeping granites of the retaining wall,
rushing bright oblongs for cigarettes, beer,
and scraggles of dry vine dangling between them,
militiamen under packs, bowed slightly
by their dark rifles, with two last children,
girl running a tight circle around boy,
a pressure no sooner stated than developed
spirally, crumpling funnel in the chest
engulfing those close strangers
                                            settling back
into themselves and reaching for something to read,
pale in plate glass we were forms for that pouring
and its planetary, nostalgic clatter,
with the two gentlemen and their activity
not gone therefore although left quite behind
dispersed and swirling, submerged after being found,
turning to the next idea and its pursuit,
going off separately though they knew each other,
deposited back there or below, each of them
humming and churning, while apartment blocks
thin and scatter and raw fields open out.

Pilgrims for Bendis

Like travellers from the last century
and staying only one night, none the less
they have returned in thin hours when fury
worked loose, landing again at ghost Piraeus

recklessly: coves were shooting white
against an undercliff, and there they moored,
scud beating in from behind. Unabated
the sea all night came heavily unfloored

and vomited morning through a coldly molten
lucidity in atoms. They filed over
a hill to the old fort, followed walls part way
to Athens, orating, shooting and roasting plover,

and dawdled where the Artemis of Thrace
had loped in deerskin, building on that beach
their evening fire. Racing for her there,
bareback riders had leaned with torches, each

a muscled glow along drumheaded air
pulsing and shredding over glinting hooves,
unlit smoke rolling behind them, skulls
socketing the flare, and then roofs

kindling along cornices, the city.
Sokrates, custodian of the chase
who came in order to see the ritual
done for the first time, saw fire wash each face

before he went back with his friends, saw flame
goading the sweated necks of horses, profiles
of new rhythm abstracted along dark.
Chines of tile shelving upward layed the levels

of inner gardens, steadily riding ship,
alabaster bloom on the slave's tree
maturing the anchored likeness, pruned and reefed
lemon and salt to the hand's tyranny

and a master who has just left her, stepping
down from his damp ledge thinking: He who died
was loveliness, but he who lives shall be lovely,
price and weight of time in a perishing head....

So that head fading will have been supplanted
by itself, hounding itself down lanes of flame,
leaving its lover wanting all he wanted
recedingly, though assured, a fleeing same.

Bendis: that sliced shining of a mouth rifting
lip from lip over those keen incisors –
has it been said she murdered with her gifts,
spear offered in each hand? They were not hers

but theirs, both citizens and aliens
together students of the kill, who lit
their many flambeaux from the one, tensing
to flare them in the collodion of spit

gilding the drypoint tautness of her smile.
Their horsemen vanished where the jetty spins
spume from the breakers, glossily rolling speech....
Between our dog-teeth hang the spade-sure twins.

Interleaved Lines on Jephthah and his Daughter

Lawn at sunset, during arrival, before the visit,
    for having returned in pride the general turned father,
not a field for crossing, bladed with amethyst,
    greeted with fulfillment, when the voice sailing out
and crisp withies of hazel twisting through hawthorn
    was his own girl's as she ran towards him. No, not thee.
Lithe and strict, that gate of a green power.
    His pledge to victory was the first who should leap the sill.
For the invitation is to bring gifts to the feast,
    the face of battle newly unveiled itself as hers,
though they could not yet pass the shadowing door,
    and the face of submission as the new face of battle.
Green at evening is drenched with the price and the consequence.
    For what should he do in some other place, with less wagered?
Emerald is not heartless, but a sunk tide of fire,
    and some other conquest, such could never be his,
jade is the pomegranate turned away, speeding past harvest.
    More than readiness unfolds the eddying sun,
unwithheld, unknotting against the remainder,
    not alone while it revolves there, nor unseen.

Fire is one, and thrusting his right hand
into it the prisoner won a new name
from his captors, the would-be killer
now Scaevola, as they watched the flesh go.
He saw a different thing, that to go on
into that zone was to encounter it
as either the up or down, twofold ordinance,

and conflagration as either the not-yet-come
or the done-with, now a fourfold pivot,
and holocaust as flanking choices not chosen,
by now a sixfold counterpoint, and burning
as the unborn who tugged him down untravelled
compass-points, the twentyfold
                                    dispersal
through false liberations from surrender.

He too saw the one thing, that he had not
lost hold of courage. But the power that saw?
More than the newly left-handed in him,
more than the right-minded, it was his full face
that turned towards fire and, though variable
and dissolving, vision finally at grips,
held that one flame as the only heaven, and lived.

Armin

It seemed an eagle, simple
turning and tall descent, the burnt dome ample,
undeniable. But what shot
    down was a shield

and stuck in the marsh and turned it
smoky and depthless. Close by, still filthy,
rearing as a hot brass flower
    out of all size,

it made midday sullenly
rebound, and I thought of crouched Scythians
when bowl, plow, and ax plummeted
    among them, and one,

coming to his wits,
grabbed them up
              and made himself their first king.
But here, only this reeking slab
    and my two hands.

Though all will come to be born
of iron and Lupa, though over the race of men
the dome shall whiten, this my tribe
    will, of the other

limiting downward eagle
bear memory and bear arms, no hotly squiring
mania ours in this pierced air
    by the bean field,

by the mucked mallow pond,
under noon reasserting its bullhorn.
I was born near hills but shall fight
    in the marsh forest.

Birth. Homelessness. Rome's wars.
January, plinth of two-headed winds,
gateway of spin-facing auguries,
    has opened on us.

Canzone of Wood, Paper, Water

Convex lens of water
in a glass is sanity,
though thunderheads now totter
no less steeply within
that clarity –
drumming in along
the horizon they encroach
on its studious thin
sweat, their beat narrowing
or widening as I watch.

One of those gestures
of useless wonder, then,
sky-clear, while a speck whispers
and flashes, rolling dark
on the cloud wall again,
little fighter
learning to search and hurl
the muddy ball for work.
Balanced now, but lighter,
I feel his whirl

in my own head, slipstream
clouding a nerve, fine sluice
miniaturizing a scream...
and can be typical
in that, or find its use,
while between acts, between
shutterings of the eye
in the meanwhile,
I huddle down to glean
the given and not die.
Across the meadow, men
swarm over a new house,
denim against raw wood.

They tap in one more good
beginning, one more end
nailed to beginnings,
in storm light seeming sharper,
brighter...and like some power
bending over the torpor
of this prefatory lull,
they fill the hour
to its brim, yes, are
accomplishers of the cup,
and under contract. A full
draught of it, then, for
the encounter leaning up

straight into the moment,
however it spill –
the straight thing without easement,
where there drifts instead
a lacey sail
spread to the westerlies
by high spiders blown seaward,
newly refined dread
and shruggings. Westerlies!
Towards and still towards,

to infect every good
beginning with an end
starved, a limit understood
too simply, and breed weary
knowingness. Or a mind
casual in its tether
driven against the marl
slabs of vapor, the very
seething of that weather
its blindness, and the whirl

of scud crowding the line
its embodiment,
the century's design
at random: streaming men
in a wave unbroken, bent
wherever force drives –
emigrants towards the earth's
stunned colors, heaped even
in their own coats. Lives, lives...
testing the worth
of repetition. I want
this apparition blottered,
for it leaves driven and spent
what would stream back to the hives
of the unscattered –

souls as bees, who accept
each lost city, rumpled
where vine has crept
crumbling them, or the trickles
from a smashed temple –
preserving none of it
yet never losing the way,
meeting the cycles
at last, sensing that it
will all come again into play.

Is it such rhythm, then,
that draws those workmen up
the roof's tarpaper lean
shingling with tiny blows
that trail through the gap –
winter brings down the year,
the unfinished house will wait
where blond plywood glows
vulnerably, where clear
showers will sop it late

into next spring. I watch
longer than I'm aware,
their work ends. Still I watch.
What is aroused,
moved by more than their care
for the god in the detail?
Like a long drink of space,
like everything unhoused,
I bend towards the gale
no longer knowing the place,
as if it were uncaused –
has the long trail
of embodiment snapped here? –

and spin like Averroes'
impulse when he first shot
our form through space
spreading it flat there,
experimental thought
stripping thought away, then feeling,
and then each sense
until the burnt-out similar
turned and flared cleanly, wheeling
into light's far suspense...

but what I had felt before
and not confronted was
my body as one more
among those roofers, held
by hammer stroke and pause,
balanced thing
meeting pine's willing pulp
with bone the builder. Skilled
in nothing more, that swing,
earth's weight its help.

Elation in flung arms,
a dancer's drunkenness
in labor's forms –
can the expansive be
driven and drenched through us
so it blurs the cost?
If only we might pay
that simply, and go free
with that much, that at most...
if it were ours to say.

I have seen newspaper turning
in crosswinds down a road
dreamily skim the burning
lake on that blacktop, light
as protozoa or odd
hints of a fugitive
existence. Whirl and skim.
And Augustine, lifted out
of things, saw each thing live
with a fulness strange to him
and felt that he had not
existed in the same
measure. My own eyes give
the figment on the road,
for the moment still ahead.

Dear child, tired father, turn
away from your play,
uncoil those worlds and learn
new fascination –
become the day
spinning more than its night
turning hard stars,
more, then, than revolving
stories the eye lets fade
towards sleep, dissolving,
without hesitation
abandon the sky you made
and go down unblinded, go far!

Out of this rotation
do I only seem to wake?
With that sharp consolation
body offers, sunk
in natural give and take,
the starling's agile shadow,
embodied world
ridged on the wintry trunk,
giddily swoops the meadow,
body with shadow whirled.
From them no one can take
the curse, resignation,
that learns surprise no more.

How long the minotaur
stared at his human hands
I need not wonder, for
jeopardy makes him ours,
he almost understands,
almost glimpses our long
incursion flare and furl
within his warring hours,
along their turnings his strong
phantoms whirl.

By Mummelsee

Down from those bluffs breeding the Ohio
one can take plank stairs, or a rickety incline;
with much the same plunge deepened and turned west,
over Innsbruck the northern rim drops you
along paths or cableway. But Mummelsee
strands you above its bowl without means.
That is a country where the half-confessed
contraction of the tongue, generations now,
has a home waiting for it, activity
festering in the ever-condensing cup
of narrower reality. Inching down,
you sense the pull of huge mass, sequestered.
Only defunct radiance towards a world
spreads from there outward, under the rocks, the waters.
A man told me how, walled in by conifers
he had felt with the draft dragging at him
tempted to pitch in rocks, cones, anything
that came to hand. The impulse itself stopped him
for he remembered a fool who had done it once,
putting legend to the test, and had triggered
a storm, dislodging water spirits smoothly
from the viscous fathoms. Though he didn't move,
nonetheless around him moved the headlong
consequence, thickening the air. Cloud fumed up
clenching, spin-coiled, its first black drops
driving eyes in the water, while offshore
frogs climbed gin-clear eddies in the compression
bubble-pale, becoming girls as they swelled
beneath the explosive membrane.

                                Then, swift chill:
they vaporized, nothing of this was his,
some other mix would measure him for his way,
without sorcery, without its flaring
blandishments. A tight hole in the scrub,
less than the half door on a railway car
when the lower gate has shut and travellers
jam the opening, waving goodbye –
that much opened to him in the steep wood.

He clambered back through it as the last wisps
of tumult soaked into air and water, still
sucking at hearing with a siphon's gurgle.
He worked into the red-trunked palings. A curious
calm possessed him and instinctively
he unsheathed his knife, stropping it on his bootsole.
Slicing into the bark, he found it pliant
and carved a roofline from the town he had left
at the beginning, finding relief in this,
and so started a record of the journey,
continuing out of gratitude. The limbs
lay out in broad sweeps, a primordial page
that he worked fluently. But then he saw
the branch above streamed with script, while below
one with hieroglyphs like a mummy's lintel.
He froze, fearing his irrevocable work,
even though the uncanny narratives
framing his own remained unreadable.
The law of their opacity, enlarging
through the whole forest, yawned a mathematic
ungraspable, unvocalizable. Looking
high among the reaching systems, he saw
phosphorous unroll a tableau, two women
leaning naked towards a figure, the arms
of all three extended for an embrace.
Ribs, lips, shank radiated through the smoky
flesh of each, Death's a bit firmer than theirs,
and he welcoming them, the half alive.
Parallel like yoked mares, the two women
anticipated only pleasure, their eyes
and mouths avid. Below, still rooted, the man
realized that any cry from him
would never reach them, shut off from his plane,
inviolable as the mute legends
cut in the limbs over and under his,
to which he could add neither word nor sign.
His knife floated. The three shapes narrowed that
sealed interval, while nothing in this world
lifted a hand to enjoin their triple clasp,
and he stood shaking for their sistered fates.

Six Stanzas in Nine Lines

The way a rope, uncoiling...
the way a loop of flax
thrashed and threading, lies over
promising a weave...
the way a sunned snake
straightens across the path,
abandoning grass and dust
as fabric to the tensed treadle
of the halted foot....That way.

Way of the announcement as it arrives, real
though only yet the real's herald, love's letters
    in hand between them, the two changing.
Way of the garden row as it sprouts, Strabo's
on his island, secretary of visions
    while sower, stem-binder, pruner-back.
Intercessory glisten of the sweet pea
bobbing under rain, her unsleeping eye
    conversant with him, her sure handler.

I crave the gradual
approximation of measures,
the way the stresses rise
from night's ground and fall
from day's flow and fuse –
Brahms in the fading ballade,
Brahms in the uprising, and
Scarlatti in the resolving
pulse, driven driver, breather.

The way balances though it veers underfoot.
Moon's wobble and the sure seasons' tread, shifting.
   Their reader twangs the rope tight and mounts.
Strabo trued lines in his herbal, sorting simples,
while Charlemagne's sons, big with brotherhood, broke
   across the plots, grabbing wide, hacking.
Orange aura,
               earth marrying polar air,
spreads for the one who reads late, who looks up through
   drifting ash slumbers of the wide mind.

Thrusting up through root veins,
trafficking among cells
on either side of a fluently
definite membrane, force
fizzes over the real.
I crave the gradual
approximation of measures,
the way a breath pushes past
its beat and is carried, rippled.

Brahms in the salvoes and then Domenico
Scarlatti in the intervening rat-tat,
   beneath them beheld powers not held.
I may achieve a garden but I plant seeds.
Spacing stakes while, spiralling, the vine fastens
   It is not magic, the quicksilver
bulge of Burgundy as it brims past the rim
and transfuses into the vintner, his hand
   that labored the one now that will laugh.

Times Passing the Breakwater

Intimate address
imperial and addictive
will move to annex experience
it glimpses but hasn't had –
and so, before our beginning, Termia,
before the claimed but unsurveyed
territory of your hair
parted across these decades, their cold neck
sleeving a hot throat and dark speech,
even then, as if you had been there,
my arm swept out in a wide gesture
to net the starched jibs
tacking and crossing –

hand isolated
in the sealed car as that mass smoothly
shot the stone causeway
in its groove of force.

At indigestible speed
Ezekiel converged
with the ballistic pellet, rolled grief word
dropped on his tongue, and swallowed.

Medicine, too, for the contained!
distributed along the urgent
metabolic fuse, into
imploded strophe and dispersed canzone.

Ignorant, what I'd assumed
but not wholly dreamed
was this: possibility as a body
naked, ageless, taking into itself
containment without limit,
curled in on itself unborn
yet with breasts gathered full to the knees
and its hands merged in devout cutwater, hair
pouring forward from the accepting nape:
emblem germinal and credal

with the sun over it unzoned,
hills and shores streaming into it
from a lifetime unbracketed –
each station of our going,
boats and their bright rowers hailed
as companions, the stranger
waving back...
that much came clear
as it floated off, lifting into view
even as it dissipated.

You had more on your mind:
through noon's bland core you were to stitch lightnings,
bread of Zechariah through his speared tongue,
the word of power like his bomber
planing in for its run.

One day, and one hour
threading the strict eye
of its incalculable instant.
Road by the sea.

*

From a late hearth
one spark, the aimed remnant,
gashes high through the gulf
its hypnotism of space, as desire
would dodge past morning: it has the flight
without the passage.

Neither as one thought
nor as two such, separate,
but as one contradiction
tensing to complete its arc limit,
we were taken up, were held
in one act of attention,
sputtering weld extinguishing first
one flux and then another
in the torch's mute issue,

21

and how long it bore
or at what frail height it quenched in a surf headlong
I cannot gauge.

                The crest highway
streams with paired humming tracers,
and closed on itself the eye spins
their homing fire, draining,
until there is only the crew from yesterday's boat
spreading their nets along
the inlet, turning to inspect
cloud where it fumed up, squiggle
on the last high cast of light:
it is they, instinctively, who'll have drawn
some inference. One mind
and the turn seaward, crabs
pulsing through drenched sand.

                           *

Daybreak vapors swift poles past the train's tremor –
slow strobe through wet glass into the stiff skull.
Your terms are not yet those of she who saves,
gentler though terrible, surer,
able to say she'll return
to the light she came from, whereas
your endings extend codas through echoes, leading
down the labyrinth.
                The signalman
coming off the last shift wades
his tide of returning self,
the numbed powers. What he hid
in the world was his effort,
hid with the unsaid and the relinquished,
his rhythm now their seal. Lodging it there,
he has not lost it.
                But your manic
scribes bend over its fluid map –
you gag the throated rememberer and inspire
interpreters, as if the savior's glare

flashed falsely over the twelve
as they sat for the first time forming letters –

to your opposite, then, I turn:
though sleep still drags down
and the wheels' gargle spills me
with every other unready and contained
through the determined curve of fall, this is
one more hour that remains hers –
what has come back to itself from the four quarters
trembles, a needle that past nightfall has held
unveering though it went with me
and with you, her dark sister,
into the clean cold.

Jonathan

Cancerous sun that uncurls, then
      eddies upon itself,
light that pillages the eyes: is it
      flood or filament?

Foremost in slaughter, Jonathan
      dipped his lance
idly into a stray honeycomb
      and tasted of it.

Bubbles from sandbars in shallows,
      waterbug flopping
over the pondface, his walnut shadow
      detonating in silt –

back, and then back along amber current
      as if I were still intent
by that bridge rail, fluid there within
      my detachment.

From a source, that flow ever newer, and yet
      at the same fixed distance.
And that is a place that I would not
      leave easily,

though the alders, burnished and pooled there
      in a fierce leafiness,
bring me to weep inexplicably
      and without bitterness.

Pressure in the grip thus easing,
      and bronze aim nestled
in a spear's trench, figure within figure,
      I would have rested.

For at every chance he had struck
      head from body,
the same music had welled in him,
      his time repeatedly

returning upon him. Hours, drowsing
        day of the brief lung,
may hear illness, another speech,
        moving towards song

as towards a dire antecedent, and follow
        over the grooved threshold,
one speed, many waters. He tasted of it
        and his eyes were enlightened.

Back, and still farther along the bright margin,
        dissolving until that stream
is neither water nor motion, and one is
        not yet among them.

The lifted forearm of even that man
        may wait upon this, may yet
forget the drone homing, the crow's eye
        poised over wheat.

Hellade

High meadow: poppy blots
mazily responsory
to our star's impress,
clappers in fire's bell
after swinging, still blurry
in the ear's labyrinth,
while dry shadow trances
the moist floor of air,
weedy, a beetle fencing
with the ant to sever him
and the fragrance of his track.

Ivy twines a column,
girds it to carry it
through close heats burning closer –
has not forgotten rupture
from below, can infuse
fibers of flowing rock
into far architecture
while hanging into dwindling
clamors of fife, drum, yell...
rout has tumbled through,
and will, while lattices
cool in the interval:
elixir and alloy
fade white past the ford,
foaming trace of a vessel
that pours further, its rim
a home for broken column
rotting trunk
   and spindle
of the jay's cry, something heard:
ivied, spiralled, embittered.

A final runner's crashings
dim around that rhythm
he runs for, dulled tumult
of his will a winking sea
pressed in its bed. And that
other who fell, extinguished?
Augustine wept over Dido,
the hymn writer had Saint Paul
weeping at Virgil's tomb,
but has the female soul
been widowed by her ashen
husband of foundations?
Through this hot salt, honey
of clarity, the distilled
engendering of bees.

Tallies

One may have lived much
yet topple plumb into ignorance –
may have mastered or endured such
    as confers dignity
    and cannot be subtracted,
    yet without dignity
    find only sufferance,

    because process reaped
as cleanly as rain-forest acres
get razed for cattle, air bases, and deep
    caves under Amazon
    for the Brazilian bomb,
    or as their burn rolls back
    paths of the trackers.

At the grave of the unborn
supreme fabulist, whole-blown artificer
of the whole effect, motion untorn,
    no elegist can stand –
    its parcel wavers, slides,
    the name urn-breaker, sender
    of light far, lucifer.

    On ziggurat high-rises
wind croons as to terns drilled in their cliff
or sailors swung near a sail's cheek, yet cries
    past likenesses, slides high
    where force interrogates
    thrusts of an anti-civic
    assertion, an as-if.

    A siren's tones
or truck tires overtaking the ear or sluices
through fever or synthesizer moans
    orient it, place it,
    whereas air is testing
    a proposition that lifts
    past its own terms and uses.

The reaching glory
alive in its own time, not to be set
back or aside, no repository,
    let it be celebrated
    by fires overruling sleep,
    startled gaze blinking open,
    unweeping, irised wet!

    Early traffic
the irritant, a young architect
leaping it, cursing its horrific
    sweep down the Champs Elysée,
    supply one beginning:
    his vision snapped, it wasn't
    the cars he wished wrecked

    but the street itself,
its inability to absorb those powers,
new torrents strong now for the gulf:
    so away with it, off
    with its fungus of the cafés,
    arbor of faces, one's own
    student days, streetcar hours –

    thus Le Corbusier,
thence our block shafts out of blank grass, a park
undreamed of by the kings, the choked highway
    easing through it banked
    under heat shimmer, sun
    a rippled orb, lanes amber
    and diamond towards dark.

    Mold the unit then
stamp replications, cost of materials
dwindling as the scale climbs, as forms of men
    clamber and grow small –
    girderwork, preformed slabs
    slotting from cranes in the dangled
    leap down Mycenae's halls.

From here, no shift
to a despot's patronage and the worked frieze,
passage over ripples to meadows, the lift
    onto cleared planes of sound,
    glow-edged flesh beyond morning –
    from here leaps aim through raking
    horns past anatomies.

    Deepness inhales, and depth
sighs out its unfathomable device –
no matter: to ride that uncanny breath
    is also to stand at a sealed
    balcony and look out
    on the weather, the eras
    as one mountain, world ice.

    (I was only one man,
I too required the protection of elves,
my birth ordinary, my path no plan,
    and for the bone bundles
    of my ancestors I was
    seeking in crumbling mounds
    for secure shelves.)

The clear light, because Alexander harrowed
the world's floor and had speared his bedmate Kleitos,
did not ripple from his cup. The wine's shallows
in night's tent, in pegged solitariness, though
clear, clean, washed towards a beach fire. From his boat
splashing inshore, he saw one of the lit stones
uncowl a face. It knew him. Led him up knolls,
sand, through scrub, thorn, onto scorified plateau
where a ground plan glowed within the rock pillow.
It was not recognition, yet he felt grow
before him the great edifice he would devote
to the full stretch of the reachable, hero's
and god's grasps interknitting, the peak off-load
of burden into governance. His guide chose
that moment to sweep him high, show their atoll
ringed with pulsating phosphor, then shoot below
to a mica-bright rock set where the porch rode
on the phantasmal structure rearing now whole.

Alexander, raising it, prayed. But it broke
in his face, a spout of bone dust, and time wrote
his term in that blast: one grows only as old
as one's temple. Brain blank, he saw his hand go
familiarly, and yet estranged also,
for the cup. That amnesia, a creosote
caulking the long crack in floorboard, hull, and road,
extends, extends. The desert general goes
in a squat tan Hummer to his triumph, so
the film star buys one, churns cloud wakes of the host.
Analogia entis! But what enrolls
memory in the electron and harsh strobes
through the mind conquering: in sunny dustmotes,
or carbuncles domed over Montsalvat, glow
of night unto itself around the Graal's float
at the peak's tip – these gleams over a cup's hollow
in the nuclear sanctuaries suppose
no acknowledgement: they wait, they impose.

        Where does the stream go, where
are people going, and the stripped trees?
For a child's ancient interrogations, tear
        stanchions loose and renew
        the wandering teacher, some
        Dio in tattered linen,
        fire's brain over bony knees.

        Wisdom's river flows
into exile, out to the Dacian tribes
through irrigation ditches that legend throws
        under the rhetor's shovel,
        though to some purpose, glinting
        while sinking, growing acid
        in the soils legend prescribes.

        One foot in front of the other.
From village wells, clear water. Purple sleeves
of memory swirling with Trajan or Bismarck: *Brother!*
        So a world has more than one end.
        The ruling mind spreads arched
        and codified, the mind
        of a Greek is olive leaves.

31

Walkers across the spaces
made for them move as shuttles through a loom
trade threads, or shattering sun changes places
    on water's noon piazzas.
    Mostly not seeing each other,
    comets and moons, they stride
    through a galaxy's human room.

But to pull one tense strand
out of the fabric, rhetor? Tell us therefore
how the lone foot, the uncontrapuntal hand
    climb solo over villas
    terraced beside the sea,
    and over deep arrowheads
    from the tenth millenium's war.

To the grave weightlessness
of Aeneas bearing and leading through pity
the fury of shattered centers, to distress
    made good by replanting one's gods,
    he adds the center's long
    reduction, he stretches speech
    over a world-spanning half city.

How a painter rambling
in his wake might figure him, or disfigure:
over scorched plains a filmy derrick trembling
    into life, ventilated
    with hills and space, the head
    a night flight's metal flashing –
    yet missing his seedy rigor.

Though he means stones to live,
dress him as he is, star minimalist,
cast him as the wind a stone's hollows give
    way to, or as late rain
    tunneling a civic
    rockface while igniting
    mica in forehead and fist.

The choreography
of a plaza, when it unfolds a place,
legs in perpetual recovery
        of falling, mind floating ground,
        actually happens,
        faces willing to look
        at no one, yet wearing face.

        Effort at ease, but effort!
What he exhorts them to, what they have listened
grudgingly for, perhaps attentively suffered,
        was what they walked into
        on other business. Stretch
        is what the muscle did
        and grab, but then it glistened.

        To teach them crystal is not
fixity but formation in the flow
of event, ingatherings of a knot
        towards ethical release:
        this stumps the orator,
        roars from the assembly
        swirling in dust below.

        Walkers into the weave,
momentarily monumental, living
curtain that rends itself so as to achieve
        a flow it ignores, show us
        not motion's decaying heart,
        but how you slide speechlessly
        into the ever-giving!

        – From there, towers winking
on in the debt-instrumented dusk, staggered
bright bits, brownish purple of the sky sinking,
        and the squares emptying out...
        there he vanishes, cars
        idling, exhaust illumined,
        and the mute faces wagered.

33

Ides of February

The flaked racing breath did not say it:
You will taste, one of a host,
the union of this age.
Blue robes hung down our white door.

On the wall Romans tussled
near the pyramid of Cestius,
heater chuffing, easing.
Brown arms piled angles and enigmas,

one body both advanced and fled,
one was the arrogant rider.
Blue on great white: ours was patience,
theirs amber, on skin, stone, air.

Danced conflict, half-sorted melee,
one of them king and fallen,
one thrust out of his city.
Snow blotted up the panes.

Each hour carves a circle
through whiteness, and a line
through time's honeyed no-color.
Between them, bodies swirl to birth.

Hours incise each circle, snow filling it,
and each line, once only.
Between, the world's bedded forms
stir unrobed and emerging,

the rider surges away,
contempt lifts him and the king quails,
an elder croaks malediction,
the new exile sees life stretch out,

robes divide white from white,
the towering pine and bed
collect blue, white, and great patience,
bodies tenderness and exile.

Circling groove slowly filling
and line arrowing without bend,
had your geometer set us
at the cut more keenly – yet

two others it was, cloudily
greater, bent on their veering
purposes, who achieved it,
blue tearing from white:

as a captain through days gazing
at butchery misted in cordite
becomes the army, while
at the far end of that arc

an inkbrush master, hour
on hour at his mountain,
the veiled life-giver, becomes
its few soaking lines.

Roman Elegy

Streets under winter rain
at the tempo of violins
scaling the end of their pell-mell overture,
pit sinking to half-light,
stragglers finding seats
as the expected thing
gets ready to take fire
in a glare of paint, palms, curled façades –

where lava cobbles melt
with dung and runoff, and Goethe's
Arcadian wig wilts yellow
in a glass niche, streaming paperweight,
a whore bends down to snatch
banknotes loose in a gust
of the North Wind, and fates
send up their clattering applause
raw heckling and damp cold –

Red managers have followed
their refugees but take superior quarters,
shake hands with the commissars of cash
then slide down runways
lined with blue buds of gas
up, into outer darkness:
though nothing that once spoke for itself
still seems to, there remains
this buzzing, this seasoned
anticipation. I crawled
dimly lit galleries
to a crypt where Ugandan dancers
in exile mimed the Return of the Prodigal
and brought one spell of silence
to the labyrinth, echoing

crossing point for power
bypassed and the long crackle
of rubble-filled walls around a suburban bomb –

she has not willed it, but her hand has spread
open through afternoon as a lizard's playground.

And though they didn't inquire,
that pair hand in hand darting
from the squall down there –
though they didn't ask it,
what has that or her other
matinée, her scurry
of sanctity, got to do with
their searing entr'acte?
Whirled in a jangled era's
grasping hunger for signs,
we were not gullible,
yet met them when they fell.
Downpour, drum and soft cannon,
tambourine trailing off,
when again the high footbridge
of Caligula rose shining
against the deluvian and spotlit dark.

Fast through that night they sheltered
and the night of Constantine,
while the blanched eyes of stunned
Philoktetes looked out
from the borrowed eyes of Rome,
a torn spread wing in his fist
hanging along the morning.
And though their balcony
dangled verbena from a smooth earth pot
breathing pale coolness, they slept in the lion's mouth.

Jaruzelski Winter

It had been a gesture
whose performance you'd have capped
with raw conviction and rude irony:
packing old clothes for shipment
in relief, the realistic
sentimentalist's choice
of one misery from the heap.

Another entire people
put under lock and key
rather than bribe and buy-off
are not being punished, they are being coldly
tested in the cold.
Even if they choose
another martyrdom,
Termia, you and I
by sacrificing warmth
may search fire within ice,
not asking for what is not
given, yet holding to cold fire.

And can we learn? The dwarf
who shadows me resists,
imagining he stems
from peasants who have clustered
around white chapels posted
in stretched fields, a figure
bent now into huddle
with an old pair in their house
perched over a river,
concrete from walls and bridges
ripping past in the torrent.
They have drafted on bond paper
their letter of defiance,
fatal declaration, cemented
with bits from Gracchus Babeuf   '
aimed at exorcism
of the bullet-headed block-shouldered imitator.
But a snowy blast sucked it

38

out the window, sailing it
into a grove of poplars
still green along the shore
where paper and leaves both flashed
into crisping flame.

   The carton, then, taped shut
over scarf, worn jacket, greeting.
Ash from page and leaves
settled across it, weightless
measure of a madness
heavy with the dear grit
from older sand and lime,
honor, linked hands, the strict wager.
Prudence lies out of sight
curving away, its pull
slower, thicker, its silts
impounding the blood and breath
of patience, a brutal shrug
millenial but not indifferent.
And if you were not here to shudder
at that sometimes wiser
sometimes harder thing,
still your removal lies across it with
the turned-away face of the time,
recoil which shivers into tear squeezing
lower than bedrock now, whole tremors
before the tremendum cancelled,
yes, refusal that prefers
to unfurl that substitute, its own passions,
and lift cold gleams
of fleeing hair over rivers
to capture the sun's ignition
on the flat bends pressed farther,
stilled swirls in the amaranthine
fire of an unstanched flow.

Begin's Autumn, after the Late Massacre, 1982

Oracles of night spilling their catch,
shucked lemons in the Campo mixed at midday
with fishgut under shut booths: one is either
weighing, throwing them out, or being saved by them,
Bruno's ash at the pole of their bright field –
anticipated fruits as pungent crosscurrent
while the cusp of an era digs in, scrapes, drags advent.

Signs of your coming, Termia, cast a salt
lemony, just, prodigal with blood's futures.
But justification is not reconciliation,
nor will the notched wood hanger swinging beside
the pan scale of the fish seller ever span them.
And neither is this momentary Rome
the unaccountable moment men call Rome.
Cloud ragging upward in a silent rifting...

remembered... thrice remembered and forgotten!
Oracles of day, sentinels of these hours:
the sill cat at drugged dawn, the dog curled
in a bucket-cool stairwell through afternoon,
while in the leavings banking an evening street
a man kicks at a console, angling
for some relic of a signal, nudging loose
screechings and then a faithful listening
in plyed veneers peeling back. Trumpetings...
unreconciling brasses unless they rise
from seen stones, and those same stones have risen
from towers that lift, evaporate, reform
through a wide arc of day not yet our home,
lift or are lifted, it seems soundlessly.

Or unless the herdsman swung bodily
by his own sheep south of the walls is not
forever the enemy – for they will die together –
of the stubby figure roughly dragged outside,
conspirators with him, agents shoving him
into a van, but not before he blessed them
with a quick stab of foreign speech.

                              The remnant
crouches to find the jewel: a southerner
kneels at a shattered facing block
prying at its focal bronze cricket,
the rot-green escutcheon of sensate life
renewing insensate luck on the caked hearth
of cobbles and the spilth of linked feasts.

Perhaps he knew you were on your way – he plucks
faster, jerks his head up, then hunches closer.

Evening leaves him at it, he too has
his mission. Evening, drawing its hazing
cadence from the unforgiving echo
given us to hear sometimes too sharply.
Over the pall rouging and yellowing Rome
at Rosh Hashanah, sickly sweet, over
the Arch of Titus Legion heaving the Temple's
golden candelabrum high in processional
pillage with lifted horns, there comes the sound
of Gideon's picked hundreds in the fenced compounds
of Lebanon, leveling the defenseless.

Whomever you choose, the hand you take in welcome
will not, in this place, ever be wholly unstained,
here where once more there can be no escape

In Lazio

Saturnian lungs
    of stone pines
breathing up bright cloud,
    and the day's
stone is adrift...

a motorcyclist
kneeling by his machine
spills oil into dirt
between milestone and plinth,

but there have come offerings
less casual, still filial, black wings
bringing down the Father's
dissociated cries, and wailings
stifled within the Iron Mother's
pledged columns.
                    From her calm
stola Plotia Claudia
reaches out a smoothed arm, towards
day burning past the next shoulder,
form broken off and the procession
weedy, gated in the distance,
past a car junked at gleaming hazard.

The family exacts
its tribute in the staid
eros of stone, its bonded
ranks and its overlapping
ranknesses
             stylized
to freeze faith, fury, grief,
bravery and breakage in their long line:
even if it's only
the twists and not the ruptures
of continuity,
where are lineages
strong enough for that torque?
From such identities

42

grouped gazing I have turned
away with a darkened eye
along other roads, but now
I remember: marking out their names
the mason saw already
the red that would carve there.

Passacaglias

Thrown swallows, called to the delirious
probate of March, declare the unfinishable
resumed and teeming among the stopped towers,
near the plaque for a boy gunned down
at the street's turning, and they shrill their choice
of the entangling covenant, although
each plummet from the topslide of their arcs
obeys a command also.
The call of matter is quieter
than any conscionable inquiry, and longer
than a conscionable care for the way. Termia,
their swoop and hurl alerted me. I stumbled
among their summonses
and then rebounded. You were still ahead.

*

Lighting on him in the throng of strollers
I felt the jolt, your invitation.
He might have just left prison:
shopwindows stopped him, all their things
he watched as if in the next wink they'd move:
umbrella handles (imitation bone),
print kerchiefs, porcelain hounds.
Taped pupa wrappings of the woman drugged
on the church porch, a boy chinning himself
up to a ledge along the baker's alley,
possessed him equally.
He was testing each latch
down the corridor, world without escape.

You invited my half-identity
with a whole error, testing the low hinge
when a door, being rehung, still
twists on one pin and teeters.
He vanished into my fantasy of Michael

reborn into a freshened beyond,
his new eyes not yet telling him
that each turn of his gaze sorts fates
not in the old way, but now otherwise.

Your straggler, sent on before!
                                    For although
he cannot get it right, still over him
up a crisp flue careening through air's levels
shot a moth bleached and enlarging,
unwrinkled in your fire,
white cell of a vigilance
willing to search high ledges in the flame
though soft, unwieldy:
                            if the sudden
were to show itself as a living
manifestation, this would be its wing,
its flutter, spreading a sisterly
protection, a frail powder
dusting both street and skull –
and if sound were to arrow up with it
clearing our hum, the harmony
would ramify, all trumpet
singleness would fray and the phantasm
fly solid:

            vibrating
strider in mid-stroke
blanching past the known whitenesses
of perishing, past the razored last ridge
of limitation, simply
as kernel of the face
unshown, bivalved seed of the opening hand.

                        *

(Cloudburst: and as I ran
down black lanes aiming for the bridge,
I felt a thing brush my leg
and then keep pace, wolfhound

pivoting with me in the turns.

You might have let him vanish
when I stopped, Termia, but he sat
waiting, a painted drum
strapped to his panting side,
the grey and red of the old Polish cavalry.

Unshivering in that downpour.
And I saw then that you were going to push me
past any chill that confirms your frisson,
past your equivocal election, back
into the ruined game.

Tomorrow when the street
channels its renewed surf,
the moons behind that roil
will send their companioning hounds
whippet-soft and cloud-thin
vaulting ahead, sharp for an unseen target
beyond the elected in his waxed limo
parting the waters with hood ornament
and covey of police, beyond the trailing
bit-players of the interlude,
phagocytes with timed satchel
lending snap to the anonymity
of shadows – past these permanent
rotations of the passing
towards that steel line which their little wheel
seems to have bent around into a stage,
on which they seem to align themselves
and seem to want to pluck
like the deep string of a guitar,
like that one string which the Greek
stretched and fingered, studying –
but forget, never touching.
                              And you were saying,
not how any of this concerned you, but
rather as the wife who sends laughter and look
from her pod of guests to her man, and then
returns to them, their voices keeping him
listening, fighting the near thing to catch

46

bits of that drift, you were saying
that the odd bond still held.

Your animal, different once more, had come
once more, not quite to remind, not
quite to admonish.

He stayed, then shot as mist through the drenched door
where last week a crone had leaned out
to stone a cat along the gutter,
but it had turned squirrel, pelted
with nuts and her rough intimacies –
skiros, shadow-tail
and ancient domestic
harvesting futures even from these streets.)

*

Bullfinch stoking his truculence,
blackcap his cheekiness: not for us
the ritornelli of divulgence, bland
authenticities of the personal gargle.

Bellied swirls of unclockable
cumulus graze across a calm
neither of us has known in long upsweeps
vaporing the mild furnace of sure days
or in the easing fatedness of rainfall.

If I spoke to my Thou as I do you
she might once more let me catch her
peering unspeaking into a fountain's bowl –
you guard the same attention and refusal –
at washed prawns left there like seeds to feast
on the insubstantial manna
of sunlight from another world.

What sky is to a soldier water is to her –
under the forebrain of the cumulus
savoring the blind bud of its thought,

he meets the overarching and just-born,
knowing as yet none of its dictates. Must
so much death die in me that life might live?

Under the brimming boundary
she locates zones where cities focus, streets
chiselled from house blocks, fluent cuts
that hold off being trued
and go on being quarried, walkers linking
hands like diviners. Bending there, she watches.

Boat near the Capo Miseno

Spur-scattered and burrowing a surge of sand:
    blue and orange down the ride of her,
tilted to hear the smashed breathing of aeons,
    so too the dazed may still live,

a painted fan spun to the dancing floor
    among the blind heels clatter-ribbed
and melting bolts oozing oxide of blood:
    so rummaging love tapers them,

    oh how the adze caressed you,
lightest curve still healing to the hand
    and the mathematical plunge
outward into the Punic element,

    caressed and raftered each city,
and in the Greek horse also it framed up
breathing beams, men itched and sweated inside her,
    outside they chanted hymns,

and now the tarred joinery of the mortises
    lies unburdened,
in the gape and roll of your undoing
    resin remembers the iron.

49

Campagna

Wavering blue floor
of a skiff in the field's river
softens a gash of red
down the slant wreck of brick,
marks the air's gatherings
where a language sank and still murmurs.
Columns, tasks, burnt sisterings
of hands torn away, towering
on the lip of sunny dust,
shag of spurting grasses,
mud of the breeding bank.
When I was struck from that tiller
it was in service, the overmastering
pulled me from it
into these alien hours
beyond a downsuck that men
much better have not beaten.
Blue fluency that I'll not
fathom, from that city
I have come back to pray you
never to bear my body
towards your beachings again
unless you set me down
with the other blinking survivors
beside the blooded stone.

From an iced basin at the window, solstice
splashed with spine sheen to a rolling fracture
of the fire entering, bather not there,
auburn Persephone bent rinsing slowly,
corona from the bowl O lucky waker!

full weave, but how could a loom have risen here?
Spindles of steel sorting sun into fibers.
Hers, but the seated one, worn threader
whose sleep was famous, foam washing years from her,
floating the treadle...she too was abandoned,
who would have thought these tines could tense and stand?

Wrath feeds on life, ire twists through mastery,
yet masters of life feed wrath without being consumed.
Spears these are, lifted by a sudden rank
down the room, hoarse salute a frame in air,
who wouldn't let them be posted to strike sky,

gather its gold along high edges, then
as one, reverse and plunge that sister of blood
where they stand, planting it to end a thing?
To arrive here their horses came many miles.
This last muster at dawn, who wouldn't watch it!
From calming water day curves up and over.

He who called blood builder is now memory, sound.
Dear, if we called blood wrecker we'd not lie,
but how thinly we should hear time's curved cutwater,
and never the full song of the falling pine,
that swish the nets make running through swells gone starry.

The steersman heard nothing, and then felt nothing,
toppling through the salt humus of passage.
And when Aeneas taking the tiller gathered
our woody landfall, the turning belt of worlds
spread out sparks of a brotherly burnishing.

Memory may work for us as did his mother
Venus, sluicing his wound invisibly,
its hurt going as a flood
                              with which he heard
one life wash over and another rise,
but faster than remembering. He fought again,

and so the other thing may not be refused,
stand with me hearing it: from the bushy hill
the sound of fellings as huge nets hauled dripping,
plasma from slaughter clotting into nebular
founding stones, and smoke breathing screens of columns.

Zürich, the Stork Inn

Before you had been brought by the forceps beak
of the common tale, before we had been dropped
by the wide-winged forestaller
of questions, the quick question
of being born had been born
many times for the asking, yet still
waiting, Termia, for your mouth
to reframe it, for mine.

   Set down beside the waters
of the Stork Inn, beneath
carousels and outsize
umbrellas, the spill of market Saturday –
leisurely miniature of what will win:
free play of forces setting
its own terms across all the stages...
stragglers caught by the throbbing or tinkly tune.
Whereas dark in your throat
gypsies huddled with cased violins
and zithers, cupped aside
from the tribes poured towards Sheol –
not harried this time, it was enough
that they played on your different keyboard.

And from the swung metal
of late summer towers, contradiction
of the anticipated and remembered,
belfries of a now,
camps and vast palaces of a sound
with no one center: from this
the ache to lift eyes wide
and hold them so, for whatever
might spring into beginning
though it fall short, through you, of the power to finish,
and helplessness, under the feathery surge
outward, to know which power may be more terrible.

Those you love you make stand
through a long vigil...so now
with the bonged bronze of ten towers concerted
through evening cloudburst
(Saint Alexander's day, though it is neither
his blood nor his forgotten life this fading
Zwinglian clangor seals)
and with snare drums of maskers
climbing towards a dragon
and gallows along a parapet,
I wait for the uptucked wings
of the ungainly bringer
to budge, for his unphrasable gift to cease
welling unpsalmed from afterbirth each instant,
for the prince of the powers of air,
earth, and underearth
to cease withholding homage from the mere seed...
thus watching one more hour,
while in the freshly wet
still tightening hemp of the noose
falls a body.

June Fugue

Down our jagged route,
Termia, you evaded.

Left to me was the plunge
through Capena, horse stairs
threading arches and faces
of the still human, unhidden,
to a ledge's burnt-out shell
with windows gaping onto

a gulf: and there I heaved
your relics, where swallows found them
inalien and steep wind
had long since shrouded the older
offering, three meters
in gold, by-blow of a god.

Channeling the wild powers,
friend of the violent,
Feronia lay masoned
where glass now cascaded
over black goat and straggling
fence line, night rising through them.

Here they put her or lost her,
tucked her in downwind,
Welle was hire bowre
What was hire bowre?
where overhead the crab
pincers its crystalline

alignment shut on your passage,
Hir bowre is of black lilye
seamlessly, although
you live more than the living...
her trellis is night rising,
thus in her hand I have thrown them.

Their bits are nothing to
the grit from your getaway,
whirling from heels and backturned
mineral glance – and still
they call you *history*,
our secular theologians?

When you climbed advancing
into the fissure, what shut
behind you was the gate
no one forces, although
the rill gurgles its seam,
pressing the cut downward.

Light going down, swallows and swifts throng,
scissoring fields, roofs, then the pine zone
and air's last pastures, grazing higher

always it seems mated, swerve with swerve –
but they do not strive so together
for companionship, they join because

both pursue the same quarry, and one
or the other will sink, roll, take it,
or flex back in torsions of the strike.

They, so much faster and quite other,
what holds them messengering here, down
I almost said, down, among, struggling?

For such balance, such fluidity
mean that the tendons lean steadily
into a resistance, gauging it.

What holds them is what must have cloaked you:
it has streamed us our time all this while,
thrusting the timeless ones next to us

in hovering passage, unfatigued.
Welle was hire dring, what was hire dring?
The chelde water of the welle-spring.

Thirty birds aimed at the unattained
and in thirty turns of their one flight
achieved range and alighted, so led.

Not so the lute player near the door
stretching behind him as a long skein
or gauze all the leafy and clawing

phenomena, all their piled strata
levitant, chiselled out, and flowing,
our world his phantasm, train and veil

for the impossible remarriage.
So she was the figure behind these
as long as I saw her through his eyes –

alma rock-hard by that filmed river
who, for all its years of sound in her,
never did lift her eyes towards it.

Welle was hire dring. Her example
was not yours: her world swept through, leaving
no rumor, and its wind has settled,

and its river has at last socketed
in its curve, so that one is oneself
listening but no longer hearing.

Past a barley field towards the cliff,
fat grasses and the early profit-
taking of dew, unclocked clarity –

sevenight fulle in the mor lay,
so her accountancy was not yours,
sevenightes fulle and a day.

   Where night has garnered day
   over Capena, tractors
   starting up with swallows,
a brown-tunicked stranger stands profiled
on the ledge fishing, snapping line taut,
   hauling in a black bass.

Where night has turned to water
lucent through the gorge,
he waits with the same joy
I dangled once over a sand bank
looking straight down on three speckle-backs
swinging fixed in the current.

The upward thread dragged by history
mounts through your treacheries towards those
fulfillments your own hand encoded –

the phantasm of your unique bond
radiates from a core blindingness
that takes fire in the eyes of many

but with grace quenches in the bass stream,
shimmering beneath the brown stranger
sevenightes fulle and a day.

Death winged and joy fishing,
winged life and a great fisher
tensing the floated line,
you have laid the drenched weight of your catch
on my heart and played your light tackle
like a stringed instrument.

Mutable lithe wrists,
tendons attuning me,
jerking along my length
as the line shivers and the mouth lifts
wide, unbiting up its wriggling arc –
finding its high, last strength.

And if Feronia were found
that quickly, offering herself
hotly? The fisher climbs
past fine limbs waiting to be parted,
lips, hills, clouds, waiting to be parted,
onto a second ledge

and pulls in his next catch,
past any offering
buried and rising here,
for she has taken more than she gives
or brings back, *black lilye, gold lilye,*
has sealed it with your glance,

the glitter in it a hot
spray like key grinder's dust
snowing from the file –
but again rising to a third ledge
he twangs the line like a bow's, he lands
the tribute, and approves.

My unswerved eyes still smarting
from grit long flowering
in her chamber, the salt
in her galaxies, I would constrain them
into paired wings, aim them above sight,
and prepare to push out.

Cento Biblioteche Italiane

Filipo Neri collared the gay-blade nobility here, schooling them in chant
    and laughter
  With a wife like that, and Chiron as fosterer, how not go far?
Intarsia books and lute, perspective lecterns, medallioned cities, for one
    man...
  One shoe off, one shoe on, that's got to be my son Iason
...while on hills opposite she strives up the goat path, laggard sister

Spawned in the sheepfolds of Hermes when that
    fleece-gold lamb's back flared
    its ruinous wonder through the flocks
      of Atreus, breeder of horses

Foyer a gauntlet of vellum, overseer the lion-headed hominid of time
  What you lug piggy-back may be a wild woman at the river, but what
    steps down is your fate
Newman's hymns drifting over the Notre Dame goal post, practice kicks
    refining loft and spin
  Forethought on sword's tip and shield's ridge, afterthought nowhere
    behind
She looks up, he looks up, their coats on companion hooks, into a future
  Snort-fire and the bull's testicle to cool him, then a pebble: the demon-
    army will squabble over it
A memorial film on Mrs Woolf, the five sexes wisping at intermission
  So oak took to wailing in the kelson: *Wash your hands in the pig*
Stale breath over a stale page: *Stravinsky è con gli ortodossi!* obviously
  Hang high the booty, a slow twirl under the thunder shaft, and pray
    hard
Rosettes on Keats' blue last ceiling, through the window waves over the
    gunwale...
  Beach that keel in the maw of Earth Trembler, back off softly
...in one sound, water in and out of the boat, fountaining
  Now we are seven and again seven: our daddy was a travelling man
Looking up from Jackson Knight on Virgil's hot-line to the muse – for J.K.
  After she had done everything for you, you could take everything from
    her
had tapped into it – I see a friend shovelling worked stone under to age
    it with worm scurries
  Follow the bouncing ball, follow the little fellow behind it, follow and
    fall

The man who savored Bentley's anathemas, at the balcony weeping,
his wife gone off
Lullaby-lay, down draco down, lullay-loo-lay
Under oak and glass, Augustinus, sirocco of African mind
Excellence herself as the matchmaker and maid of honor; what then
went wrong?
"Ten minutes on the ladder, like a large closet, got the accounts, then
tea with the Duchesa, and the door"
Magick him away – do the demo, then slice him and ram him home
Elephant in the portal cornice, apse window past the stacks: Malatesta
For neither med school nor law school, yet set aside after getting him
through
Hope Not Nor Fear: but make fast that book trellis with wedged mortising
Send the pretty thing a new robe, and put some feeling into it
Van der Weyden's gentleman with an arrow, two red slashes through
the grey vane
Send your children to the temple of the wild woman at the river
purchased then lost the same day, left in the locker and poached
Seven and seven ripped from the altar and stoned: let Euripides retell it
Knight of the Golden fleece, pelt as brooch slung from its noosed midriff
Mad Herakles awaits the touch of your red, your black, your golden
hand
Gold carcass with hand sleeving the shaft sketch the heart's pyramid
The last interloper, unfixed from the stone bench of hell, packs you off
to Italy with your snake primer
Passing beneath the left arm, it has crossed the core and held fast
Like Helen at Karnak, you have a last rendezvous with Akhilleus
There is no extracting it though the gaze drifts far, pooling brown rain
Like Hebe the unstained, and Faust the blasphemer, you lodge in the
glad pastures
It cannot be lost, has penetrated and now lies over, the grip easy
He turns away to returning love-boy, she returns to father and
recrowns him
Arimathea's ladder at that angle, corpse slung sinking, risen
luminescence

—— • ——

The dove flutters contrariwise through the harp of porportions · mineral
refraction: bright travellers warped to the loom's frame

—— • ——

One boot in Hades and you're due back there · columns tenoned, altitude
tasking their footing
Valtellina and Val Camonica · walls in the House of Aietes
One page, gusting sorrow and wide night · louvre those clerestories over
the Corso
Hands aloft in prayer, sun aloft · arms forked and fire also reaching
Inter pres · two ceilings from two lives, the equation breaks there
Larches rain on the stone map, doodling it gold-orange · Etruscan then
Latin
Your lady's poison but your name is medicine · over the lintel, twined
serpents
Fields, roofs, wagons, ox teams, recorder of deeds · decimals saved us
Stuccoed headstones dug from the garden, our door · *inter alia*
The sickle moon on Falera's low stone, eroded · humidify the *Physics*
The zodiac cupola's jungle rot · light reddening in the hair of fleeing
Berenice
Swordsmen facing off on raked raceways for ice · lettered lintels,
numbered stalls
Monops, monoglot, monosandalos · plenitude in a point
Strike high fire's dangling rays, and a hand greets you · buttered
thumbs on Bread's vellum
Hair shining down his rube's back · at the coat check, gleaming baldness
Water in the moon's saucer, aligned with sister stones on sunrise ·
stretch and rise
Sun's home and dim hall of invisibles · that white head cradles half our
catalog
Five knives and eight parallels new under the sun, berry stalks and
stag · focus floats and so gathers
Escort from the hel of Helios, that girl-Odysseus, his fire in her veins ·
gild the bronze Psyche
Magnified I frays, the groove's ridge stutters · *typus*
Vellum yellowing insensibly · scissor rocks nipping the last dove
Plant a tree, raise a child, write on stone · water, bark, rag, hide, acid,
gold leaf, berry juice
Lectern pews for praying shoulders and impenitent knees · Herakles at
the oar bench
Knives laddering the rockface · her wedding prelude a clatter of un-
sheathings
She will empower you outward but not to delight · marmoreal skirt
swirl
Orfeo accompanied by drawn swords · plough sword stoneword,
verses epos script

62

The central steps ripple, flankers holding fast · Orfeo tipping up the
    hatch cover
  Lump of earth my milkmaid · "You clasp me? For your children's
    children I am home."
Converted church, stacks brimming, time's catamaran · keel laid by
    Athene Argó
  Solar sisterly stares, Kirkē and Medeia, murders emerging · candelabra
    in both corners
"Well, buried another pope. Let's get some coffee!" · Deathbed at rest
    in the archives
  Miming the moon's curt circle, troughs for blood · margin gutter
    margin
Rustle of ledgers and poplar tips · Orfeo to Apollo: Crystalline passage,
    please
  Even before mucky Chthonia went sun-bathing, Aion was mixing and
    matching
Dry stench of bindings, Phineas' food · Apennine thermals, Rietian
    breezes
  Quartz veins through the image · chevroned angle of reflection
Dragon vomit and death's vanquisher · herb-smoked scroll unrolling
  The Son down from the cross leaves the cross · corpus down from the
    shelf leaves the long house
On both seas active, the isthmus sleep · sun cresting on PLATON every
    January
  Codex a cave uncoiling · stone cerebellum labyrinth, death as seen by
    the sandal
Portage through twelve nights for three women · time's keel is lettered
    but the sea's eyes blink at nothing
  Kirkē's Italian hearth scorches off homicide · uncial obits bound in
    pig-skin
The Son of Man led the Round Dance · whirl of the twelve above caves
    burgeoning with amethyst
  The walls whirlpools of gas, within, blindness · equinoxes a fever chart
Spirit's fierce ring but only while forming · nape columning up out of salt
    sheens · or resolving back to the stranded and twi-handed
  Flint's channel · quill's wake · subacid superiridescence
Swing your partner · round she goes · cross-indexed raftered ribbed
  Ich bin Kristall · the boat's strict rib your skull's hammer · angles solid
    content variable
left right · above below · on back · leaving homing
  Roseate · dodecahedral · smaller than carbon's ring · in and out of time

Little Frieze

A fig bough sprung by December rains
    over a garden wall
from the trunk that cradled and remade Mithras
    scrapes on the rim of the solstice.
From storm scudding above Rome,
    from lungs of a mother great
in Israel, sea breathings drench
    root and wrenched limb
and the colossal rose of a trunk ripped through
    to yawning fragmentariness.

Standing to its knees twenty days in Tiber,
    it, too, sought castigations,
the city, pursuing its immortality,
    shedding mists, the grades
of the Lion, the Fathers. Soaked cold, it dozes.
    Newly, storm tunes the world.

*

Looting fury and torches:
    sheeny cuirasses hovered
        in the smashed portal,
five rays fanning in as the flat steel of swords.
   They stood sweating among timber shreds
   looking in along the probes of that steel,
   walls high around me, terror unswallowed.
   But then with muffled drone,
For one thousand years, for another thousand years,
the spread of a crown claimed that glare and upheld it,
   broad silver in the tired house of blood,
   flared prongs in the glad seat of blood,
Through one thousand years, through another thousand years,
and the fading chink of stonecutters, and the dwindling tread
    of women bearing them water.

Huge light, calm pool, and a great dawn shears evil,
a sky lens, as one mind, lasering it –
but overfull, shattered, salt Isaiah or Ezra.
So the raised voice went awry, the wind took it.

Now from Potomac to the old land: the Pershings –
new angel gave not the hardened but the mobile.
In one contracted room curls her prone form
while space, wingless, extends the vast lily.

Below, circuit and angle propagate
in fragments of wheel rim and axletree
while night skims overhead with their iron pattern,
black quadriga tugged by foam-lipped breathers.

The sleeper, still real, dear, ephemeral,
neither withdraws from the messenger nor draws near,
while the city, not yet returned to the dust
drifting down on it, floats beneath the reins.

*

   The trap lies open, entire
and sunbaked in mosaic and statuary
   jagged along the cliff:
   a caesar's hand in the craftsman's
and grass whispering, more than ruin, engenderment –

   renewals green to a steep mind
that as will would be blood and as best blood
   itself would carve the clear line
     hodiern, modern!

Yet say it: that whole drive
gets put down less for arrogance than for going on
   speaking inside, and listening –
   as if at a stream's bend
sieving wing glitter over shore grass,
   lute's bowl and geodesic good
   tuning the lines of transmission –
against the headsets on picnickers over the site
   or blaster boxes whanging,
this vast revoicing pressing outside, immune
   to the trap's fine teeth, Quintus –

   say it, but of course
   keep it to yourself
     while on the wall's edge
     at the garden's end,
cooler than the stone images,
pants a skink, pausing in the discourse, his skin
   that of the sea far below
   in its calm agelessness
barely wrinkled, breathing slowly.

               *

Let the high grass caress
saving errors with the wind's hand
and keep the lines of transmission
open.
     But is it easy
to man the lines when the operators
have taken to spoofing the notion
of getting anything straight,
and dismantle the switchboard, and
issue bulletins about
the filmy nature of testimony?

The antique bomber rumbles.
A bowl on the table trembles.
Sun is a pool on the rug.

What do I look for now
in the long push of river,
coldly living head
anchored like a salmon's
sculling within that power,
anchored over shadow
    rippling its bed
and fluid sun of an hour,
    net that takes
gradual gleaming hold
bending, and shakes out fraying gold.
What do I swim for now
in the pouring length of river?

Cries weave out in common
from the hawk-shrouding tree.

*

As with a spark blown upward,
dangerous, sudden, clear:
a city swung below,
Ephesus, its far bay
and a yard where silver burned,
smith hammering the Graal
still early in the day,
bell sound, shiny crack
threading cores of suns
packed humming on a wire
curved close enough to touch –
then silence in the colonnades
when Apollonius turned
halting in his speech,
stared and stabbed at the air:
Strike at the tyrant, strike!
Domitian dying in Rome,

67

god there and here, the dreaded
inadequate god of two aeons,
submitting on the small
anvil of a man's reach.

   This in one roar
over the world away,
this from estranging height,
our demos frightened or blind
or both under faint cloud,
while the half memory
of some cold, clinging fight
sank to a darkening floor.

                                    *

Warmth at the long window
out of the blue split wide:

a man planted his cane
into cobbles, peering right,
the wine seller flapped
faded yellow tarpaulin
free of dust, a girl
jeered at four men playing
soccer by their shops,
a red-skirted woman ran out,
her mouth clamped across pain,
a crone lifted her finger
toweringly along the sunlit
ruin of her face.

Facet of the stone, flashing,
that seems to give life to me,
yet this is only half
the grid, and the jeweller cleaves it
open with a dark stroke.

*

I stumbled from a wood
of pillars to night-soft fields,
pressure of the others
behind me, all of them known
but closing to what stood
fulfilled and rooted, deep shield
and shut leafiness of brothers,
while out of steel beaks a music
curved off in steely thread.
Knowledge drained out of me,
heaviness flooded back,
life blinding through the head.
From that changed city a strand
of wolves' eyes glinted, no sound,
and I slewed through black sand,
gained returning ground
as they drew in, their wiry
shudder the rim of a sea,
and swung around to face them,
but faced an immovably fiery
grout of stars, the tree
and vault again of heaven.

Three Little Odes

Auguring come the phantasies of a boy
who though becoming no builder knows transepts
red as the underearth of Pharaoh's temples
furrowed from sandstone, the sea's crumbly amber.

Under the fate-winker, high, hugely fallow,
the blueprint of our seed has lodged in halls
judgingly neutral, where an effigy
plows up sleep with man's hands under man's head.

Explanation goes on through the long watches,
soaks warmth from the mute fires. But already
when they were children murder thrice renamed
silted their air to stone, blotting the patent.

Bryhtnoth at Maldon let cold sea harriers
unimpeded achieve the dirt causeway
being a fair man, fatally he let them.
Loyalty, estuary fog, men's cries.

*

I gathered my childhood songs
far from my birthplace, in eroded Carthage,
tenements burying the moist
bulk of uncarved tribunals, mossy blocks
dripping rough Caesar's rust,

where I heard again the crumple
of the rotted beech back of me on a hillside,
when the crash made me cry *Domine!*
Not quickly do men cherish their walls and rooms,
and travellers take their way.

70

To be alive now as the
custodian of momentary escape
    is to dawdle after the first measure
among pediments edited by sharp grasses
    nodding towards the shore.

    When the present bells out to a bowl,
a shell of oxides, enamels, airy forest,
    then the month called nine falls eleven,
and throws down its shields along the steep path,
    and lives wherever driven.

    To be alive when the tether
of order has yoked the sun and severed it
    with a stroke heavier than the legions,
and the oak of Subiaco stands vaporized
    by a thought, the unknown imagines

    but the flesh will drive to know,
will ready itself to harbor, and not hold off,
    nor chant the fallen trunk upright,
nor call the swallows back from their long homecoming
    to the fire swinging from sight.

                        *

    Not one of the tragedians
drew the knife through Iphigenia's neck.
None of them was able to haul that far
    her slight body. On the altar
a meteoric deer bled mountain blood
    when men dared look.

    And the imponderable
weight of her betrayed promise they hurled
delicately to the outer limits.
    The young bride dwells in black Tauris.
The separated lamb grazes grey rock tufts.
    It is far, the world.

                        71

Far while flowing through, its orbit
arrowing up within diamond freshets,
pouring with animal tact through bloodrush voices.
    And so I shall set out for the straits.
The rumorous stages, the sting of the Black Sea beaches
    will not outreach it,

    the shore will unlimber, jamming close –
the last approach, guessing her gown's salt fleck
from that long thunder, quickly over –
    and the first touches will mass, meet,
the frail, granular, shuddering green rock,
the grey, greatening, ponderous, fragile wave,
    fuse in the shock.

Turns near Vincigliata

When April
gusts through mold-marked cypresses
lending tough sprays to flame shapes
along lanes girdling Monte Cerceri
and a flag iris ripped from the wall top
splashes a nova
over night-shining curves of road at midday,
it has begun to be far;

when paving stones
mound through returning rains
not so much as cameos
or ambers through the flash-stasis-flash
of a carver's lamp under the centuries' wet chisel,
nor as the hermit crab's hump
through tilted sand runneling silver
after the wave-suck, his canker
the clamp of a back-tugging aeon,
nor even the multiplying
curves of blank wakings, not quite stone not quite eyes
neither a street nor a face,
then the span has stretched far enough
to take the measure of more than trudged-out aimings
and to pull them all, as water
over paving stones, tight and straight;

when rooflines lock
into their habitable puzzle
or genially crazed plate from the ridge,
singular angles nestled and absorbed,
it will begin to be far yet still
condensed around the renewably
outworn, winking on as air darkens –

even bridge piers
on the far rim will collaborate,
letting ungraphable
convergences poise the cone
of remnant fire on its arches
and two dolls flat along the span
to bear a towering figure, neither future
nor evening's vast figment, its wide arms
not to fall until what has passed for life
has been swept by its updraft
into its imponderable stand:
not all those weddings we have forced
with Death the Drummer, our
demanded certainties, but itself it offers
in the fires it kindles and veils,
blesses, it seems, the pair there,
though whether they give human place
to its height and pressure is obscure,
they lay there because for them
there could be no other crossing.

Not for them the climbing glitter of our near shore:
we shall be known as the ones
over whom a flood of the unlasting
swirled its picturings of phantom
abidings and bright cheats.

For them, seeing has been changed: the readable,
replicated in a bland light, grows arcane
while under sun's weight the encrypted temple
raises its profile on a near wall.

The soul does not need many images – the needed
impress bites and takes hold
with sounds maybe of speech
maybe of demoniacal or divine
flutings to be disentangled,
or as hands have sometimes etched it, the winged sayer
not blatant but muttering to her
through a wall blind and mortal:
if lucky, a sound
fringed like a philatelist's window

with the gentians of mint issues,
cored with the shifting glossiness
of phenomena over frail perforations,
all of it to slip towards whisper
and be far enough, the valley past
uncandled flames at the road's bend
fathom green and then lighter
under the clouds' passing.

Animula

Hotel window, and lakeshore
mists throwing lamplight back,
yellow of landing lanterns,
into the room until
a boatman snuffs them out.

   And this immensity
expanding through the black
O little one, this thing
in pang to begin to live,
swung by its feet like a bawling
Petrarch, what use will you
make of it?
               When the shine
of the high hours goes, a man
may seem to give steel to his years,
hands welded to the wide sill,
yet gapes like a child before
the dark auras
               flaring –
may seem to have come
to a new footing, watching
couples from the boats
trail after children at the lit landing,
yet stands there under the spell
of the hint, the requirement
of our hard second entrance, its keenness
lifting the snail-wet umbilical
sheen of far inaugurals,
no longer far from this shore.

Before a Journey

Laying down small branches as a kindling bed
for the lopped giants. Piling them into thatch.

Their bark rivering the palm with a cow's tongue,
their weave roping childhood muscles over shoulders.

Crossbracing the topmost ones with fatigue's blessing:
though no meat roasts here, there is procedure in this

older than the last ice, its curtain through this valley.
And the hour stands over against us in grey robes, Abram

with reaching rod: *These cattle and sheep I scatter,*
herds of smoke will remind me of who I am.

Beginning the burning with deliberateness
and no voice, with steadiness, seeing whatever greatens

among the feeding tongues, knowing I have stayed
to labor for them to the end,
                                  when I might have

pictured more completely, adequately,
ungovernable dangers and so cremated this present,

might have tumbled with others from the suburbs
after the prophecy, sermon, mass baptisms, tremors,

and the vermilion cloud dusting Constantinople,
streets unechoing at midday, the Emperor

and his bishop camping in the fields. Last branches
pour their forms out boring down into blackening gold.

Border

Swiss bunkers on the Rhine,
weeds bearding concrete that bears
plank marks from the forms
to shade trout fingerlings
nibbling in shallows, leaping

and we have found the leafy
Roman watchtower base,
four vanished stories, and crashing
through have startled hawk wings
widening out over the motionless
fieldmouse

        There is incalculable
speed in the floating thing self-contained,
weight hanging in empowered
patterns that have not yet unfolded,
which even those who have lived out their fates
have feared
        so is it a hope
that may go farther,

          hope for
  life of the path
that goes out, that looks up
  and is not crushed –
down that path farther
  or the wheat track
a German farm girl had made
over there, Swiss widow now,
made every time she hid
her friend at night, a swimmer
either side would have shot.

Kayak Island

From their shore into the curled race
    they push off, battling foam –
    slim prows finding aim
    while helmets spin and shine.

Bright primaries, fibered resin,
    aluminum, impact plastic,
    with timing in the trellised
    nerves, the inward tree.

Bobbing in line, hovering where
    rip eddies buoy them,
    together they wait out
    the rhythm, alone in the rush.

Each cycle one or another goes down,
    righting in a slow pour –
    we push out but go also
    into, into and under.

And then back – the risen spume swooshing
    around one buried tone,
    men and women recircling
    through their insistent image,

working it deeper on crumpling silk,
    restamping it in melting
    silver, in forming pewter,
    founding, establishing.

Yet where we clung once was a ledge
    rimming the tideslip, breached
    curb to the suave returning
    surge, the great opponent.

Where we came who remain scattered
    though watching, was a place
    where brown kelp sometimes lost
    their holdfasts, and went out.

Blunt margin of a binding law
   whose teeth whiten and drain –
   blunter than fear at being
   called out of the known.

To have been led out is to leave
   each other to that leading,
   where periwinkles smashed
   from their rock crevices

will make their way on a piled swell
   to native height, and grip,
   come back from their diffuse
   endless captivity.

And we are cut off, we begin
   to go forth secretly
   out of confusion, many
   are those who must go forth.

Somewhere already they are leaving,
   their feet sound in the small places,
   the ear hearing them loves
   that going and waits long,

waits long through the attentive pause
   whose gatherings are farewells,
   whose psalmist is a raw
   scattering of crows.

The last fleck in the lifting flock
   maintains two intervals
   tenuous and electric
   with earth and with his kind.

Evening Concert

A swollen pink hand shakes with palsy
but the trio sweep it into their current
where it lives, master of the meter,
mute interpreter of water.

As in the tales there are two of us
yet everyone else is at hand also,
transparent to us without our looking,
murder with love in the lull before pizzicatti.

The violist steadies, and brotherhood
spreads from him, his companions nod to it,
for these are the kin privileged by twelve deaths
under moons no man has inventoried.

The one who feared his own will to heroism
but came to a martyrdom new under that name,
newly hidden from our sight, stops
his bow at the steep end of that phrase,

so that the scribe, Entangled Figures Master,
who insinuates Job through a vine arbor,
can cut through it all with one stroke, and where
history stammered a listener now leans forward.

Polimnia in the steely gauze of Cassandra
disshevels herself in a whirl, my heel-sharp
Polimnia who then tucks one finely
clenched hand under her studious chin.

Even in the last cadence, spotlit,
a tripod of pine burning by the doorway,
night planted near it in striped pantaloons
and those who came to hear entering in.

End of July

Of longing, Termia, the sharp specifics know
no end, and down its progress the sharp days
lose no edge, the hours
crumbling streambeds to strand
the source deeper in summer. Orchard ladders
lean into the moist sheen of dark globes.

Near Baden under swallows, one
belltower cut through vineyards, banners out,
when the wish fixed me, rash
as blind archery, to lift
one clean impulse streaking out of the ruck
even if it landed wide of your touch
while quarter-hour strokes
through worn maroon face rings rounded
on their gold mark.

   Slow tones, swelling
things to a lightness – but if
that shivered me, it wasn't from forgetting
how separateness the cold angel converts us
to our fixities,
nor from denying she turns
each of us in her fire
like hickory seasoned for a torch,
nor from ceasing to share in her trade
of thrust, chill, thrust, the injustices
giving and taking justice in good time,
no one shouts the recognition,
it will not cry out in us,
yet they rang out, bronze
minutes, the bronze years,
with blunt frayed rope those changes
threading the spin of one swallow
who still climbed slabs of vapor thickening
over vine and crest, then
targeted down through harvest,
his poverty with ours
uncancelled yet his riches

plunging, sounding there
while bolted counterweights
thudding inside their dry tower argued
you could not hear, and claimed no one could tell you
how they made medley, before the orisons
of Roman candles and rocket wails
broke from streets below:
Unification Eve.

Fantasia on a Theme from Don Giovanni

A Jocose Apocalypse in One Movement

Bring the strings up from nothing,
    violins from the sands,
from stone powders for the justicing
avenger who promises a fire
that will set all right and cure the heart.

Sets fire and holds it and wields
    his rapier of care,
blade of ages a quick floodlight welds
to hot feeling ever returning,
high motto of Don Ottavio!

A knight's pledge to the besieged
    soiled soul of the world,
the betrayed spirit in silks and edged
golden nothingness without which things
sink to lead, ooze to the final mud –

pledge sealed by snorted or yelled
    refusals, espousals
of *No!* by the ranks and rich, one guild,
revolutionary quandary
when at last headed off or bought off...

we've waited for you, sir, have
    longed for you with dull pang,
though each heave of our animal love
trails the rakehell Don through his pell-mell
descent and pillage and abandonment,

trails him, anticipates him –
    our master sniffs the air
and we take the contagion, the drum
guiding us at wrist and heel, ruckus
of blood repetitively wedded

to glad eternals of mood
    gladly delegated,
happily feathered in haphazard
changes of role, though we'll see it all
inscribed, oh yes, we'll chart each sad bed.

Brahms stayed away and Shaw stayed
    farther away, rather
than watch the radical thrust downplayed
to the jovially curial,
its low triplet of protest turned cute.

The relaxed second cellist
    with her small part, alert
to the stage, smiles up at a new tryst –
and yet her role is not marginal
if she lays down her bow and gazes.

Two musics from life's two books –
    marrow of the mired bone
whistled forth into astral statics
by the mouth of rain, then man's long tune
whose constants get woven as one dance

for the three orders, gentry
    and pass-thoo by middle class
and pipe-shrill stompers from the country,
woven as hum for the Don's ballroom
enthrallment of a pledged peasant girl....

But the force of a dark farce
    pressing real darkness
from a whole order into one man's cries
leaves out our armies, our furnaces,
summarizes no red horizons.

From the Sea of Marmara
    one stone inscription
cuts lines far into a tomorrow
Mister Zarathustra told Mister Nietzsche
to watch for, tap-tapping at his door:

Oracle of the Sybil:
  when Dionysos
shall have dined to his satisfaction,
then blood and fire and dust will be poured
together. So then, good luck to you!

while the Church had its stones curse
  badness with harsh goodness:
VIRTUE FEARS NOTHING OF ITS OWN FORCE.
Can you step past these, knight, can you hope
to innovate for love? Though it's late

for love wholly to remove
  its supercharge of rage,
there is time for the steeled voice to move
iron law in its own heart, and draw
more than hurrahs for tessituras.

Idolize you though we will,
  give you the stride of a god
as you approach, like pylons in file
across our hills under great cables,
you must remain human or go down.

No difficulty
            there! You
  will most likely carol
coming revenge while making soft-shoe
shuffles to the rear and a side-door –
our cynicism, your realism.

(But the unknown makes a suspension,
while the known confirms it: our version
can go only through the end of the first act, leaping
where the stone father has not been, and go on hoping.)

The second cellist, her hand
  resting across the strings,
mutes no smile, she will not understand
anything not amorous, and not
hopeful in the end. And she's no fool.

Those furnaces, those armies
   out of paintings, came out
of an eye so far within it sees
from a high cliff, to the lowest shelf
of fiery dust, through the still-wet past,

to its last zone, the open,
   the unblinking, the wink's
density of now
                  infusing then...
where
         the first ones – the pair at last
meeting – under clear bells stand mating.

A kiss on the shore of space,
   curl of the wave turning,
green-windowed comber rinsed clean of mass,
of forest slash-burned, of shafts deepened
under ramming arc-lamps...yet no dream.

Kiss no kiss will inherit,
   earth given unto earth...
water loves the low places, spirit
has gone there, and we into desert
no more to damn the red earth that is Adam.

(Goodbye Leporello, Zerlina,
Donna Elvira, Donna Anna,
swift interchange of faces, Masetto and the Don,
motion out and away, Norma, Margaret, Tam Lin.)

Sundays, German villagers
   gather on knolls and hills
by the Autobahns, to watch the cars –
old and young lovers as spectators
of all those others, the bright rivers

slicing in close pass-pass, phased
   procession, recession,
lulling and agitating the gaze,
a vast circulation without rest
not quite festival or spectacle.

This is no city, this place
    between cities, the sheen
of glass and metal and a swift face –
this is a step out from that, a leap
past the walls and gated terminals.

The Don led his parade down,
    to be sure – absorber
of essence into his heaviness
the way a stone sinks into snowbanks
with the sun's weight, hurrying black heart.

Through Dresden, skies of London,
    through flares of the long fire
at Alexandria, eyes undone
by the fall into their space may pull
evening from evening, going

out of focus in the deep hearth.
    Yet a glow may show through
the altering floor of the betrayed earth
the way wheels take form in the ice walls
of a cleared mind at its blue demand,

shine as the ground's own vision
    of itself to itself,
plain thing that will be a hard doctrine.
And so shining, like the steel-bit line
of the engraver, it may give her

a seed picture, no summa,
    and desolation may
rest as the plane of return's rumor
trustworthily, not for unearthly
restorations, their cloud salvations,

but as rudimentary grid,
    spokes of the wheel awake
in a first motion, an unhurried
leaving, with the woman and the man
tracking coolness through the heart's distress –

winding to their city, bound
   for the edge of all edges
at the rim of western fire, the wound
of all light held by its towers and healed
by the many
   beginning to speed there
       over land and sea,
    beginning.

Stanzas from the Bridge

Darkening the dome
of Peter and the castle
of the smiting archangel,
swifts in churning billows
    finish October,
revolving without sound
through the eve of All Hallows
    over Tiber.

I number my own dead,
but while these clouds wheel
I feel a change of scale,
dilation in the breath
    and time's working –
more than a thousand, they
will not scatter to death
    without larking.

Suspended, blankly lifted,
I watch them weave confusion
layer on layer towards precision –
the near ones fast and black,
    the high ones slower
and grey on the hypnotized
dome of the open. They tack
    and dive a full hour.

A man with radio
pressed to his ear stares up,
a widow in black cape
buying tomorrow's flowers
    squints, holds the view,
and coming home from the flics
through bankside sycamores
    lovers look, too.

Who among us has seen
the thing? who alive
has numbered the beast that will give

its sequence to our days,
   what our days saw?
These don't tremble while tossing
and shuffling the fierce maze
   of the hidden law.

Gladly, now, they're embodied,
the tiny and terrible
cohesions of the small
levels, the burning bonds
   airy in things –
silently they are bodies
pouring out along glands,
   bone hollows, wings.

Men and women alone
who sometimes become seers
of terror the Alone shares
feel only brief terror when
   giving it greeting –
feel that unspeakable touching
go through and then on like spun
   galaxies meeting.

Hours beside a candle
before the cooling dream
had consigned hours to time,
that was a time for learning
   the way these play –
flecks of soot swimming hotly
to the sipping wick, then turning
   in bursts away...

if I'd looked up from that
and at that moment become
what I now am watching them,
it is the pale flame in power
   I'd see overhead,
swimming unreadably
above them, this tall hour
   of the living and dead.

Hours near the Crossing

Scrawl of vine across
the doorsill: last night's storm.
White stone in white sun floats it,
   an undisturbed
puddle of stony fire.
Surface that seems above me...
and then, steady trickling –
that would be the catch-sink
in the next yard, its pipe
dribbling a silver runoff
from the still-drying roof.

Odds and ends of the trumpet's
eternal aftermath.
So the baton slows, hovering.

The boy who cannot stop
staring down at the beggar,
and the slumped form itself
inured to that look, stirring
not from shame but discomfort –
these are the stricken stem
out of which curb and doorway,
windows and eaves now spiral
in a choked blossom.
I have waked near midday
to scooters in the cross street,
unstiffening a shame
prodded by that bronze hour
whose heat inwardly thickens,
and stared over terrace walls
strange in that instant, past
bell tower, muffled cornice –
have gone into that gaze
as blankly as the moist
breath of the foliage
evaporates, or shadow

soaks into stones at noon,
noon stunned in the submissive
heart of over-use,
Strength, Fidelity, Nile, Ohio,
and so out to the rotunda
with cupola and cross
wedged among twiggy aerials
and tiered roof gardens
to see two workers drift
undizzied from behind
its windows, navigate
their catwalk flattened out
by distance, and disappear
into some nearer wall.

Glass breaking and then laughter –
a rabble of carousers
drains through the night, where down
from the window each is blotted
swiftly, although still
trickles of abandon
silver the great cave:
this is a taste longer
than echo. And their strength
is to drink quickly, hear
only their jangle strike,
tinkling day into blank
with deaf sweat, deafening
effort rinsed there by that
    brotherly numbness.
And a hearer dumbly drifts with it
when he had meant to listen
further into runnels
of the attrition, goes out
    while his clay darkens
at the cool window, floated:
spun towards high deltas
where the weave tatters out
and momentum unravels him
at the dissolving tempo

of rains, containment, patience
into the gale's long curve
flicking at the scruff of matter –

blacker bitch of the crossroads,
moon in your tooth and hearth
in the smoky geometry
of your throat, from a whelp
we have known you and yet only
in the weight of having done little well
do you press home.
                    My dawdlers
draw to your pelt like iron filings,
simplified to your vast underbelly,
smoothing until the street
crushes to a grade shot with morning
and calmly rigid figures
have turned, their work in bundles
under their arms, their shadows
cleanly monitory...
not yet the two realms gearing
fast, but touching; not yet
the achieved but its guidons.

So let that wall angle
thin to the garden behind,
its rank courtyard lapping
the plug stone well, brimful –
where no splash came when a finch
dove from one side to slice
that blue, his font and mine
in a pact too immediate
    to revoke now.
And strength not to be claimed,
strength of the keen forerunners
unrepeatable, all
poured out, let it be spread
as air burning across
those slopes that lift themselves
above their crest each time
the eyes dart up a fraction,
white ribbon of the after-image

and quick curtain falling back
over the noetic chink –
while the bowl of clear fire
remains to be walked into,
each crinkle of mislaid
intention reignited
by those small knots of people
taking cleared ground above
the city, at the pace
of conversation.
                  Strength
poured out yet trembling there
through every category
some have kept molten: hope,
the several just rages,
the fatal pledges.
                  It need not
be wrong to have been strenuous
though inadequate.
                  A bald man
tumbles awake from his roof chair
where the heat ripples him,
disciple gaping up
at tumults of shape – maybe now
he will hear the command
fashioned to his one need
and his renegade role: *Kill and eat!*
While two streets over the bar for
young fascists, and not so young,
cranks up in custody
of their own portion of light
and fair play. The capacious
hearth of strength! No poker
needed where the ember
cracks open to burn to the core.

Out through an underground
corridor they led me,
one on either side,
into the arena, those seats

of stone rising in their huge round.
State officials waited
with secret police, the talk
American, Israeli,
German, Latin, and clipped Chinese.
Dusk high over Arles swarmed ungated,
another had just been led off,
So finally, I thought, *it is going
to happen*. In the center
an infant, his flesh corpulent,
ancient, greeted me with a cough,
the sound of it vast, broken
inside an avalanche
or coal down an endless chute.
This goes on through ages. And then
they let go of my arms: I had spoken.

Pebble into air,
and the boy's hand cupped upward
and death not yet mature
running after.
           Birth with sun
pouring, and in the square
the common bread lies scattered,
eaten in urgency,
stupor, or a blithe
unconcern for what comes.
Nocturnals into day,
a full weave not forgotten
but not sung through, the whole
singing not wholly woven.
Death with us.
           And the mongrel
sure of his rounds trots past
with his morsel, delegating
care to the willing.
           And I hear,
not the clang of harpers
striking up in places
where the women draw water,

not that plucked gut nor yet
the plashing: but a faint
doodling of winds and strings
down in the luminous pit
as the milling audience
begins to flow again
   towards plush rows,
houselights about to climb
down their long scale to darkness, the white
   under-rim brimming
with dawn at evening as the plotted
spell of shadow floods up.

Rhapsody for the Gatekeepers

Alas that was an encampment where I had bivouaced too often before
  reporting for the first time.

So that warders required no password and the barrack-allée of winter
  poplars whistled up my intent.

Numbed and skittering from me: piety. Through flickering documenta
  strewing my discontinuity: piety.

This was no whirling fatigue of a strict passage followed by its clear
  fields, but a Suebian stone rolled shut behind me in the embrace
  of blank acreage.

The expulsive sword of flame bent back on itself at portals where branch
  tips nuzzled spurs along wire, perverse similars.

In beerhall windows masks wobbled on, blue fur sheathing icy tusks,
  and through their heedless warmth I smelled boys' hair, defense-
  less.

Vessels calming in coves, landing parties foraging upcanyon, had dwin-
  dled to naive predestinations, trellises down June avenues, in a
  crystal lattice whose interlock was all our sky.

Ranked poplars sentineled a ducal quiet while snow squalls in reverse
  tremolos indulged the sentiment of time.

Filleted, dispersed guardians, did you swirl past me towards the child
  straying on the soccer field, did you gust over punished olive and
  juiced green and the jell beneath them swarming like choked
  elegy?

On the cinerarium of unrequitable ash, white had melted but clung to
    ground and wall.

Cranes spindled over fresh housing while my wrist spun reflexively,
    this and that evanescence where bared necks, buckling once, had
    granted to the ongoing a precious narrowness.

And over these the tent pegged for a man's measure, sheetsteel of
    sentinels withdrawn into the longer watches: thus to tend or be
    tended, where the difference fractions into aftermath.

Riposte

No, don't ask us for
the heart as heart stood once,
don't expect . . .
           but I've heard
the bells of Cerveteri,
bells of Tarquinia, and
Fool, I said, *be quiet*,
neither dominion, prison,
nor single breaking of chains,
thus populous, these are
the bronze thymus of courage
and resignation, long
interfering intervals –
no pope or Krupp to melt
their pulse, unchangeable –
while the folds of those tiles,
squares, tufted fields
roll out unharvestable,
irreparable, forage and wall
of seeming's harsh rumors,
of a held sound that hangs
out from us and colors
and claims the sometimes still
intolerable throb of body.

Weather over the Lake

Bowl that lifts roof and path into one round,
road and roof brimming the bowl with living, dying:
morning's wide breath relinks patterns on water.

Lights in the factory at sun-up, hull lashed to hull at midday.
From strictest quantum simmer and along foamy rock
probers lean out, finding the next ford in the river.

A shuttering of light from behind, grey going grape blue.
Though I went on working, the hair on my neck frayed
like cable in the museum, flax from the Stone Age.

The creamy paint I layed on that man's house, which tarp
kept off his cute little Max Ernst bronze, had been mixed
to resist dawn shadows, noon shimmers, and now this.

Black sheering up while the powerful say, *We lack power*,
roofblow from a black root blooming icily, flashing.
But even Alexander poured the one full helmet into dust –

for a shout can break forth in which any cry wakes
to limits, and the drums be uncased in acknowledgment.
Though it reach our tongues, it will be spilled, every drop.

'Siete voi qui, ser Brunetto?'

Not the Polish physicist
asking for help with busses, he
a new trusty tugging on his long leash,
but a Palestinian
who swung against me from a hand strap
downhill past the leaning
tower where tales fix Nero
during the fire, blurring whole eras, crooning –
out of all those
identities jostled on their way through,
nameless, this is one I have tried to name
when the face even of a master ebbed
across the interrogated dark and this one
hung there, like its own star, over no ground.

The Tiber synagogue, thudding
helicopters tilting away from it,
had just been bombed. Better a bus than the street...

The squares past midnight, tame
as the moon, lull with their amplitude:
when I swung out to scan the slab of high chalk
inscribing those from the neighbourhood swept up
in the last massacre, a car shot in
whipping the inches behind me. Fading radio...

But it will arrive, the longed-for
vanishing-point prick through,
far from the tracked place
or haunted wall, will finally quiver out
from a past crushed till it must turn future and
twist living through some inconceivable knot.

That spring after the quake which levelled Acre
a traveller to Nazareth
equally hard-hit went into the church
eyes full of ruin, and he heard
preludes, swelling chorales, and then he saw

the organist leave: a ten-year-old Arab boy.
Will it be such a fine inversion next time,
would it be scorable, even – the dispersals
incalculable and the penetration
of a jewelled theme to the chance ear from thrusts
of air, of tremor.... Face in the dark that stays.

Livy

When the Leader's orders came down –
  Blow up Paris –
the general cleared his desk
but left each bridge, every stained
roost for Abelard's pigeons.
And so they patrol cornices,
gurgle, strut, it is they
who change the guard over that courtyard
where a boy frowns at dust
ploughed and mazed by hunkered, persevering
Archimedes with stick –

thus the geometer, the sighted man
  not yet effaced.
It is still a mortal's
privilege to encircle
with hickory or linden
fingertip, deciduous point of the mind,
young feet exploding through that dust, those patterns
when the short sword, when the tank track
fueled by Marcellus comes driving,
the consul over Siracusa
at halt as he looks out from
the love of cities through tears
manly to preserve her.
Spelling each other down
the watches, astronomers
listen to the night.
And that year the sea caught fire.

Dearest, Infernal Granite

– Akhmatova, "To My City"

I guess, from report, conscience's effect
carried like coppers on the tongue, paid in full
for lexica carried milk-like in the smashable
pitcher, vessel of clay, singer, I mutter,
but learning how to hear in that name a sounding.

Depths, I say, dreaming the lead dragged through silt.
Mist drifts through lamp cones in the parking lot
flat on market slab walls, shiny on the cars.
No fisherman splashed loose this muck, no bowsman
exploded it with his line. But these are our shallows.

Here swim now the lights and the half-lights
of the expanded world, spectacle for its god
which to gaze on brings blindness, which to steer
among gives slowly a counter-sense of homing.
Towards the condensed world. Through the ever-converging.

Seventeen Years after the Tet Offensive

Not the wasp's cycle, but the cicada's.
Jellied fire afar then and rage near,
the form we had sought in furnaces as our ward
repouring, beaker to beaker, a corrupting flame –
this as backflare to dinner among candles,
guardian lindens, mullioned seals over twilight,
where the host, healer
in wineflushed age, bellowed,
Not men, but viruses
each year withstand onslaughts
and come back stronger, more inventive –

in the long line of change
they are the winners, mere crystals!
Candles in line, and seasons,
as metal somewhere below shifted its melt,
crusts rupturing red-gold
and boiling through the vessel lances of air
still climbed among the flown
ladders and tried arbors of pattern.

Report from Mendrisio Station

Candy wrapper blown
        in the freight's wake

No longer to be gulls, twisting
after this thrown bit or that
while the crimes harden

The platform at Foligno
another July gave a blind
veteran, medals sagging
his lapel, lifted
onto the blackened local –

here one does not stand speechless
in a circle of yatterers,
one simply stands speechless
for a long waiting follows the fixative
gaze of the sun withdrawn
into hazes veiling hill rims,
a long heaviness invades curve, angle
which has not yet become gift of ground
        not yet wheel, rose,
bronze disc or the shut lids' blood

for those, those revolve here
where clattering through shiny
points the donkey switcher trips
empties and a brakeman
leaning an orange vest
out from them drops
snatching a clip-on red lantern
from what had been the end

110

Causerie

Exiting rue Bonaparte I might, for a wink, deceive myself
as if trailing Theseus up from the stone bench of hell.
But no, from the outermost province, distended acreage
of an idea's plantation, I traipse with light baggage,
yet even so I was here before ranked floodlights
were set drifting past these embankments on scows,
their green bow lamps turning the muddy wash fauviste.
Faces ranged on twin decks, galley rowers
suddenly unchained, dazed as the smutted Louvre
flares up with the phosphorous of their passing.

If the real would yield to broadside scrutiny, illumined.
If loudspeakers amidships could amplify the hidden name.
If palaces given over to the many might truly receive them.
Ramparts of the detestable and cornices of the desirable
shine out and recede, rhythms of the strange.

From outermost centrality sped on the backwash
of an increasing acceleration.

Seining fish from broad lakes, inching down factory
smokestacks with troubleshooter's radio and brain,
combing threads of microcircuitry, my blood
regulates no maintenance of elided *de*
nor ancestors forced into the manor garden
to take their meals while sentinels of the new order
saw that they dined plainly and not to excess.

The long lane debouches onto wide frontage, winter sky,
journalism, thin chapters flapping in river wind.

Aging, Jefferson wheezed beneath the plaster
hardening into his life mask and so was not heard
in those rooms he had designed for his children, jolly
confections of classicism and styles quite contrary.
With him, the only such rooms. But beyond his cry.

If posters did not float the vanished, Dali's starved
Elephant of Space prick-eared and stilted on spindles, burdened
with the obelisk of Poliphilo and Bernini.
If Bonaparte had not penetrated to the core
of the pyramid then returned blanched, resisting.
If the masonic eye gleaming from tomb's tip on the dollar
were Sarastro's, flute handler and president of hope,
initiation master of marriage, gowned in corpuscular red.

For the pulses of a sure artery, into the capillaries
of a future, not the severing of a vessel.

My aim was not to feel again the squared granite
shouldering this flow and scan cold revetments
dividing it under bridges cleared by wily kings,
as if I might arch back and retrieve thread bedded
in the labyrinth and return with a dripping trophy,
returning so as to look past the hooded gaze
of fur-capped Franklin, instrumental man. Nor was it
to emerge into sky vaulting the spans, here
the last monarch, thereby effacing cycles
and foregoing the trial. Here again but at harder speed
mortal gates swing back on the deep whiteness
of the underworld, inviting anew the lunge that could
carry me crashing soundlessly through its vapor wall.

Riddle of Peace

From the bright tip
of his bill,
his bony little
lip all yellow,
he sang it,
the little bird:
through eleven
centuries and more,
bald cleric
looking up
from copy work,
and out of the future
breaking open
over stone
chilly in the sheen
of the beach,
he spoke
one note of it
above the grey loch
from the cover
of a heaped branch
all yellow:
a blackbird.

And from a wing
white and far down
in March scrub,
unheard though singing,
self-thrown
over the rooftree
of Francis, cool cave,
a wing quick to see
from the blown knob
of Subasio,
a small bird:
from the burn
of that white falling
a breath
of the same telling,

while the climb beneath
that torn air
was also a climb down
to the sea at night,
the sea hard at noon;
from the slight
passage of the bone-
colored bird: a dove.

Frieze from the Gardens of Copenhagen

Towards a train for the city, a wrong turn.
Ships, drizzle, islands
and the blank Strandvej, and a high wall –
rising there white heads
over white breasts, karyatids,
and the hot jump of a band pumping Swing and Blues,
tuba at the end of a sweeping drive,
hospital staff, and a conclave
of diabetics under umbrellas: they had wanted
and gotten their serenade.
Nurses told me where the station was.
And this was Dagmar's house, Queen of the Russias.
House of the widowed empress when
she wandered home again. Low scud
and laughing brass dripping where they stood
and telephone through the lab window floating
in a stainless steel
cradle for beakers, were the fairy tale.
I found the train, and walled faces,
and walls that merchants had laid on the cold sea plain.

Then schoolchildren questioning:
Why does Mr Muir say
"stretched him on a rock"?
Is "him" this crazy man?
Rain had veered to sun.
Sun also estranges
the holdout raging through sewers clubbing rats,
thinking he drove back Ajax slayer of cattle.
Rats skipping across the scurfy hills,
"scurfy" is "skurvet". Dragged
into stony day by robbers.
What is a "smooth sward wrinkled"?
"Sward" is your "gronswaer",
and that green spread is our garden,
dollops of peace puffing the cloud screen. *"Him"*
is the old man himself, his fury like Priam's
but he lies there without a name, resisting
until the thugs have killed him,

115

the figures writhed for them now,
wrestling, the young readers
forming those lines cleanly.
So this is how you will tell them?
Perhaps they already know,
although their fathers only
pretend to tell them. Ask, then.
And from their tongues a curled clang
Under Troy's riven roots,
"riven" we have too in our language,
another resonant room
in the city long since leaning
and holding into sea wind,
Where is the treasure? one girl tittered while
green sun smoothed out the blue
of sturdy delay, blue time overhead…
but *riven* is where they take us,
those of the seeing tongue:
fractured ground, and raw heat
crisping the blown branches,
divinatory hazel
hanging over its lip,
and holy mulberry
singed by ire of the updraft.
                             Blue overhead,
but held also in eyes searching eyes for
the color that listens and is still life,
over, under, sheen beneath treasures.

2

Stitching up the loneliness of stretched space,
weaving the web of times, one wanderer
made Cassandra predict a blind Homer
crawling as beggar among the burial urns
to hug them, have speech with them. And so
cellared his way, on a woman's tongue, to all
the first disastrous dead of song's long sunlight.
But force is now. Sunlight is Lykaon's
one blink longer.

Descent calls out now and
out of the years swept down I see the skiff
    I rowed to a house when our creek flooded.
No boast, this is my way down to the dead
    flickering in the blown moment.
In waters to the southwest a Dutch captain,
    ancestor, swung his merchantman
into the wind around a knot of boats
    bailing out in the storm's wake,
and formed a lee pocket in which the British
    lashed themselves to his waist and so were
hauled on board. A routine measure to meet
    freakish extremity, nonetheless
he was rewarded with a key to the City,
    that empire flush, his own waning,
and I do not know, when on his houseboat tied
    near the fork of American rivers
he looked back, how that glistering bedded
    in velvet, notched for no rude door,
worked in him against the wash of lanterns
    lowered among ropes and hands,
or whether those impressions are my own
    imposition, a fond surplus
kindled to give myself a torch and way
    with sentiment that would pluck one man
from the tight weave of service and hard profit
    to thinglike forces, and save him
from them to which he gave himself, to which also
    he saved men for more years at sea.
    I cannot know. Those are two lights
brought together in the reducible,
perhaps discardable glory of circumstance.
Yet one of them is rescue, a white fire.

3

For those who were never in it, luxury of the god's eye,
as Neptune's at Marseilles screening it from his green floor,
    each hull a pod, its petals
fanning sunlight, slow oars,
    each pod a solar rose
        self-igniting, tar flaring,
bodies a pollen drift weighted with armor, trailing
        the slow mass of the reflux.

And because only a handful heard Homeros;
and *Faust* was read chiefly for its hi-jinks;
and because Melville moldered, came Vietnam...
one wakening or another for those who were never in it.
        But we are in it, alright.

Sunflash seen from a freighter, humming black flower, floating
big chopper, petals flashing,
    petals fanning the air.
Probably it was ours
    or if British, a Lynx
        with Seaspray screens, Decca panels
equipping the Argentine over South Atlantic,
flower of the fascist pampas drifting in sea wind,
and the god's ear listening through a U.S. Creditor
passing those officers,
    The last two on that trip
tight-lipped Frenchies
    our own Flying Nuns....

And for those who were never in it, view down onto spread waters,
numb participation not to be avoided,
    we are in it, alright,
        it has never stopped,
cold blast of the door draft, splayed limbs
    as the forms fall, a rippled
tearing around the human
        fact diminishing.

4

Not knowing that a tower stood there until
 lightning sheathed it in a long embrace
  down to the trail, and its one window blew out
hissing platinum, I stumbled and froze
 not knowing any longer where I was.
  Then his dark form stood against paler dark.
You're past the forward area. Get back!
 One step and everything turned grey, ground
  and air seamless, though he retained outline.
Yes, his own hand, it wasn't line of duty.
 The other one not in your family ended
  in bed, the guilt crushed out of him by then.
Both of them had clouded my sight, but now
 even though he could read me I grew calmer
  and saw the long spears of grey grass below.
Pick those. Eat them later, and they'll carry
 into the places that will never quite cure,
  and root there. They resisted, but came up.
Their scent of earliness, their silky toughness,
 suddenly made my cheeks stream. I pawed at them
  with my free hand, and my mouth surprised me:
It's not the patterns, past or to come, but how
 to match one chance for birth with this eruptive...
  He set one foot on a ridge of turf that grew
distinct now. *This, always, has marked the precinct*
 for lightning laid out by the augurs. Rome!
  A buried nerve itched after prophecy
yet one of the two dead men formed again,
 the tougher one, artillery officer
  who stumbled across unarmed enemy bathing
after he had been cut off, holding them
 with his sidearm for hours until found,
  cloud going over, river going by.
After this abrupt tang of relief, hunger
 to lose every tension tore at me
  more than for food and drink. And more unmanning
than tears, the impulse to chuck hope with fear.
 So, you hanker for clarifications where
  you see already, knowing already the test
and even the part you'll be called on to play?

119

If this grey murk got any brighter, you
would tease yourself into luminous numbness.
Dug in on Coastal Highway One, a friend
  got through that year by drinking beer laced with drugs.
    Face drying now in cold wind. *I'm not here*
to lead you to the brink of somewhere else.
  Even if you name me – "Know ye not me?" –
    you'll backtrack to a phoney breakthrough, wanting
a sure thing all the same. For whatever
you may have perceived in me is no way out,
  whoever you find isn't me. The grass fumed off,
and the way fat held near a fire slides gleaming
  to an ooze then shoots down sizzling, his form
    sank through sheeny oranges, blues, and rippled
crackling into nothingness. Exploding
  laughter creases darkness the same way,
    bits of that shimmer hung there now, one like
Napoleon's head at a Paris theater
  childishly dozing in his future's promise,
    then sheerly alert, then senile with depletions,
time's three faces parodied by power's,
  flattened by stage glare, neither flesh, wax, paint,
    nowhere itself, yet one of us; and then
another swung towards a notepad and began
  framing terms, as the verse essayists born
    again in our day – Hegel's lank hair green
with jellied flame, Herodotus in the eyes:
  Thus for their sake I now speak not at all,
    he chiselled, and his phosphorous jaw boomed,
It is for their sake that I won't speak now!
  The head fused with its molten cloak. *I do*
    speak, but it is not at all for their sake.

120

5

Famous, the nostalgias are yet are not,
for such powers, if construing them as such
you take them to heart, you are not, of such
powers eating at you, you are not yet.
Of helplessness before poured misery
you may not be, and of forgetfulness
if it drip from rock numbness, neither will you,
although you hear them all make festival.
But the head does not hold this, and the heart...
but the heart cannot hold this. And the eye?
The stunned eye blinks open stubbornly
on Ptolemy's sun, its dear up and down,
practiced in forgetting, little juggler
leaving his high toss to fend for itself...

no, requires the main figure, hungers for
a brave conspectus, two-legged, bearded, striding
in the unstill swirl of worlds shading his eyes!
So the ear clicks after the moralist, tapping out his
walk up and back, down and up the main street,
but the aeons crave stillness....
So the ear rejuvenates him, illuminee
in tattered stripey cloak, swinging a staff
bellowing at traffic, king
of that tornado, how many years Its unheeded
authority? But they jam past him,
aeons floating away.

6

The one whom I met? Take him for one among others.

Two boys had lagged behind their school tour,
had taken the wrong fork,
and evening was reddening snowfields
on the peaks, so I doubled back
and took the other road, and saw no one
down six turns of it,
                    when he stood there.

He had seen me first, for he watched
to be sure that I watched him
set down the blue wheelbarrow
to which he had lashed two posts
freshly barked: *By God this is hard work,*
and wiped his face with his apron.
Jawohl, hard, and then stumblingly,
with gestures: *Have you dug the postholes?*
Yes by God, and that was the worst part,
water coming in through the marl.
Makes this part seem
                    even harder, Yessis Gott.
Days unfenced towards evening,
one field and one path,
and if you had gone looking for him there
would he have come? This is the gentian's hour,
the outcrop's vapor, stone set aside
in unmarked allotment.
Have you seen two boys? and I signaled direction
then pointed to his posts: *the size of these.*

If you heard, even if you overheard,
their speech is not yours, their speaking
is to no one.
            No, Yessis Gott,
but if I had you may be sure, Mein Herrn,
I would not be carrying their little brothers here
all by myself, and touched the peak of his cap
and went towards the dusky crown of that turn
and over it, before the pair of them
jiggled back, yattering in the distance.

7

One could stand on a sea cliff before the house
long since mortared there, and know himself one
by fronting all he had ever called the sea
with all that his nerve had raftered as his own.

So that place stays. But if even heroism
alters because the torque of it, twisting
out of a spiral, pressing from it whole,
is a blind blue thing turning in the chasm

that is sea, and is space, and is a new house
shaken, all intermingled, and with him there is
no similar, and no tomb loaming
his novel landfall there, what is our case?

We would not stay with him, even though
we'd cherish him no less. Nor would we look
back along the high bending courses.
Nor scale down the cliff. But we would not go,

for there is a mouse burrowing in that field,
wintering in the stone cellar, listening
to the sea bash and scour and to the man
in his sleep moan and in his prayer weld,

this persistent, most moderate brother
who will make the necessary accommodations,
hearing tunnels meet and the grains ticking.
He, mouse, go-between now, ambassador.

8

For who were the companions of the one
                                    hounded by gods,
the one who lost all companions? That is not
one of time's inquiries. And the dawn-gold ox
swings down a long lane towards fleecey space.

And space seals up sodalities of the sparrow,
beetle, and cornborer in its cross-barred
orbits of whispering stalk and canted ear,
until one white hour of harvest harrow.

123

Ah, then, a stone tower on a salt meadow,
laid up by hand on that alluvial palm...
but no, towering rushes sway bent there,
grasses and stone streaming under flood shadow.

9

If time is the wife of water, and if space
is the other wife, the dry riverbed's,
if stream and bed have sistered them, then how
had the one spread and the other driven the man,

nail head and hammer, for that was the print of him
    when he came down the trail
still seeing what he had seen, his arms stretching
the dusk wider before him as he spoke.

The look, too, of one who had survived
    events unplaceable
yet pervasive, finding now his valley,
descending into testimony still closed.

It was in a ravine, as if twisters
had flattened trees in rows. Men and women
    strewn in a dead peace,
clothed for the cold hunt or a late wood walk.

    But fear neither drifted nor hung.
An ash blonde lay sheathed in green, burgundy, cream,
and a blue wool innermost, nearly black,
against her nakedness. Staying by her,

it must have been a long time, for looking up
I saw a wall turret, one window orange
against evening. And with back to the pane
    sat one I recognized

not from what life gives or withdraws, but what
  shrouding, it waits to show –
the wall deep as a dam's fullness, and she
reading up there, turned away, calm and warm.

As deep and as ready. And then I knew the bodies
under my hand would never be wholly strange
when I remembered them, although, always, splendid . . .
and through them the sea's sources, pouring north.

10

Past smugly boobed sphinxes
at the Dane king's hunting lodge,
herds of well-to-do deer.

Kestrel and kittiwake
mingling in a sea air,

an eight-point buck stripping fuzz
from his rack on a 'phone pole,

and down from the lodge sea lanes
past twelve acres of grass,

and deer rarely shying,
strollers with liquid eyes

in pairs and clan linkages,
cyclists abstracted, fauns –

this place is as good as any,
beeches in low spreading clumps

and shadowy stands, to begin
the accounting again.
                            For here

the lull, the lay of parenthesis
in sweeping but struck phrasing,

125

is a calm too assiduously
preserved to remain restful,

passed over by too many wings.
This is the lagoon.

Then a lizard peering up:
Attendez, this is not quite the place

you may think it is! And I nodded
in deference to his seniority.

Nothing personal, you understand,
but deposits should not be left

uninsured, the management has become
notorious for its fudging.

It would have been an affront,
asking him how he came there,

or inquiring into his ancestry.
He sensed my tact and ventured,

Betrayer, and destroyer,
and now you're turning the knife

on yourself? They will live.
But differently, differently.

There is much humor in this,
as I'm sure you have confessed,

much that is ridiculous,
irreplaceable! His eyes glistened.

Pouring through forms, a peace
that would not end though they would

made the cloud-swish of wheat-spill,
of a scythe's way-making

or voices dimly clamorous,
pushing a little group

out through a gap in the dirt
under his breathing feet –

so peace was going to be set down
in the windy book yet for good –

a widow sickling her lord's field
up and down one long day

in order to free her son, and
finishing, she fell down,

my intact lizard grinning
as he reclaimed the acre,

its colors wheat, sweat, and sunset
under the blade's hard breathing –

hush, little Four Legs, don't you tease,
you have led me far enough –

and where I stood was stubble
on the berm of a raised path,

where I swayed was cleared ground.
Peace will try many forms,

Abram and knife and ram
and she who was each of them,

fabled but untallied
where the doe arcs and slides.

Space, the dying stag, browses
in the wood of Charlottenlund.

Grace in spotted flesh
darting and the wide light

that returns, leather tuck
of his mouth not yet anticipating

its red froth, and over him
breathing's blue lull

harboring the greatest
fundamental, expectancy...

a pruned and changeless zone
ruthlessly to be changed.

Kestrel and kittiwake
planing in from the sea.

11

That which does not pass but returns to peer in
    from the top corners of earth's hand-painted page,
little moons looking down curiously, little suns
    looking down blandly and benevolently, for these, too,
there is laughter, inaudible but presumably full, a long chorus.
    Was the laborious hand innocent after all?
How did he manage it, this durable cross-section
    in the colors of berries, a breviary of muds?
He discovered something. What is it? Behind the gold leaf
    it stares and winks, behind the stains also.
As if waiting for a response. Though what can one do?
    A man's lifetime tripled, clacks the stammerer, that equals a stag,
three stags give an ouzel, then three of those an eagle,
    mounting to salmon and finally the yew tree drinking three gulps
of bright dust to span earth's age on the rimmed octavo.
    Merriment ripples at the corners of fire's mouth.
And the fair daughters of fire, hair cascading their treasuries,
    nymphs outliving ten ember birds, choke with pitiless delight.
The one to whom they consistently attend in the great garden,
    the one they relish most, is a climber with donkey.
Undulant pebble nudged up the crest by heat shimmer.
    With him a boy, slaughtering knife, and kindling.
Do? Even the being of the wood is unintelligible

to the strictest simplicity: at the fuzzed edges
of imagined weavings, drift your growth, fibers,
    and unlock, unfold into the full amplitudes
of your reach, and to your unclaimed auras go.
    A dense thicket, bees resuscitating the hive,
bundles loughing against ribs and blown flesh sacking.
    From the plain below, the crystalline rowdiness
of a wind band starting up, bass drum pacing them,
    lighter than pulsebeat, the clarinet rippling upward.
The rest of the strenuously recommended procedure?
    Huge bodies dragged across puddled lines of altitude
and beached at the appointed minim by more than volition.
    Dimension thrust and cinched through the pack strap's eye.
Feelings framed in the throat's pit, only there, in that gristly flower.
    Reason coming in, as it must from its ardent nature,
on wings with an exigent, an already created ram,
    dear reason in the dress which it gallantly adopts
out of passion, the partisanship of creatures,
    parliamentary gallantry in a moment without rules.
This one is sober, cry the high ones, he's no mere belly,
    he has done it, has really lifted himself to the first step
and is going to follow through! Then more laughter,
    whose attitude is not open to scrutiny and whose
unsearchable quaver does not yield to long study
    as the knife is taken out and used: thou dost not.
As the fire is kindled and the wood makes rendering: thou art not.
    At which the climb may invade calf and thigh, memory with forecast,
anticipated descent stinging the chest like woodsmoke
    at work in the persevering eyes: so he has accomplished
this thing about which the stone is speechless, crackling wood also,
    over which the soaring chorus also flies speechless,
done it like a man up there on a mountain in Copenhagen,
    over the gardens and sea. And the aeons of light were still.

Ars Poetica

By silvery increment, by mineral touch of the remorseless,
the irregular stone takes shape, though it derives shape
from the ruled lattice, denuded hegemenous crystal.

The bitterness of salt is a taste waiting to be changed,
waiting with the power to change every other savor,
dissolving under patience of the rains only,

like the rich man's regatta fading down evening beneath
the outflowing half of breath, towards the pulse's cusp,
and masts creeping beneath their spar candles.

Round

Belled ink and umber, shouldering
needles and humus, pleated
flesh earlier than ours
gilly near deadfall after rain:
inverted flasks and cool fire
licking down from Pluto
tongueing them with solving
showers near sunset in March's underworld.

Whence this clearing
opening through mind,
fume of cut grasses, wet stone,
granular manure of seedtimes
abud in the shadowy inane?

Opening with the persistence
of an aging Samurai
who thrusts off a welter of coverlets
shared out by his rook-and-rust-haired
companion sleeping through dawn
in the drug of her youth. No one
to see him reach for his sword
without looking and calibrate
dripped rhythms from the eaves.
As out there on the grey
silk of advent, its *plisses*
sliding, so here in the day.
Looking into the sidefall
coil in her neck, he knows
that his long dalliance
has woven no ornament
but sought the basis, yet also
that his death, circling towards him
from the forest, probing mists
across the chalkline into
opportunity,
would prefer him like this, trying
to get to the bottom of it,
sword hand hanging, gaze in the auburn pool,

still trying to get to the bottom of it.
That is not his way,
anymore than the unexplained
vanishing of the demented
boxer Kleomedes
in whirls of fists and blood,
into the fading cult
of heroes. Greater images
there are, but are not here.
Past the end, honor or dishonor,
the thing he was will be swept
into incalculable
enlargement, keenly hard:
therein the mature assignation.
He swings towards the converging
adversary, adjusting
the quotient of welcome,
exacting from it the testimony:
thus was it to have rendered
account in those mucked years.
Swings away, name and face
rounding to the zeroes
of the bookie, but we say:
    he achieved
in the reign neither of Akragas
nor of Finn Broadhand
but of Wen-jo Ice Eye
scanter of food to widows,
and to that degree the luster
    was the more his own.
Behind four pines on the ridge
the fireball bulges, darkening
less, melting its solder
to the crest, seeking
no basis nor avoiding
an application, but proceeding, proceeding,
as the rust inkcap at his knees,
whole in his hands, lifts with them.

Why has he spun and fallen
in the perpetual flurry?
fighter, yet unprotected.
Crouched thighs listen, studying
the afterburst: yes, how?
Time winding in the fern thicket:
shrill of the last oriole
as dewfall shrinks the heart,
then from the peaty floor
of hunger, with lunge
skyward through the stiff swale,
those drumming wings. The sound
enlarges the cicadas
months gone, their legendary
test of our conversation
compacted to this single
stroke through our parrying –
big wing and huge flutter
to assay our persistence
in asking and listening,
clatter and the thing's gone
into low hum abiding.

A messenger starts from the point
ordinately hidden:
this is no new-fangled song.
Ascending spirals he draws
copper fine as the rinse
of flame, paring alembics,
blown snow withers
through the skier's cheek, he has
regained the aperture,
his speed is the egg's,
                              the pouring
ridgeline soaks evenly
into his glasses, and the sound
pits and drills their black slopes
drenched with the heaviness
that he sheds now, going
    out of the mountain.

How begin? fret the sceptics
over again: it all
comes again, hugest wheel....
But have they yet descended
to the hobo frying his catch
nightly under steel spans?
offering brew as tart
as might the disinherited
could they gather and pour it,
tins over spidery fire
clink this inaugural,
their delegate hunches down
stirring, no mutterer
nor shifty waster, he swirls
the layers of their hours,
in fellowship he offers
their endura: take, drink.

Neither pearl weigher stave shaper
humped track finder nor squint
genealogist of forms
the genie springs from the point
hidden in, so as to manifest it:
this is an old-fashioned song.
Ascending
        the horn's bell
                he draws
copper fine as the whoosh
of flame, paring that spiral,
for in his eye's nook a wind
feathers from summits, a wing
trails vapor and the beast
spins forth, slipstreaming wet fur,
a flank wound licked to silver
unfurling its pulse, or riders
moving into the luster
of their steel, polished mist of armor,
passages sunken in metal –
nor does it stop there, children
link hands, centrifugal
days bulge out fired colors,
the beast would reach after but his

talons rebound from that nova,
and their cherishing him begins then.
Cruelly begins, as blown snow withers
through the skier's cheek, he has
regained the aperture,
his speed is the egg's closure,
the ridgeline soaks evenly
into his glasses, and the sound
   blears from their curves
drenched with the heaviness
that he sheds now, becoming
   that mountain.
This is the ring of hours,
a same and different metal:
touch it, the tone tapers.
Across it through afternoon
fat flakes drift
into the open mouth of this realm,
one million melting, ten
welding and holding. As when
a man with a boast on his heart,
or a cursing, or the prayer
that tatters into argument,
lets it out: flakes of it
swinging down the gulf
and stitching the tongue with cold
repeatedly: no drink,
but over the dark months
a matted reservoir
contoured to every curve.

Ring of hours that hums
with planetary subflux,
interswirling streams
through magma, their churnings
brighting all that dark
and steadier than the drone
of cicadas. Stymie or
still them and there could be
no gambit for Mr Franklin
trotting off, interest fetched
by a twister over dry fields

135

growing from spurts of dust:
They say that a shot, fired through
a water-spout, will break it! – and canters
into the skirts of that turbulence
thrashing it with his whip, eminently
and passionately curious;
not heedless, nor meaning
wholly to straddle that fracas
from which his horse shies, none the less he
reopens the game: three miles downwind
and leaves still settling, what is it
that has come into separation?
He will wait upon it.
As under, so above. And as
from tins over spidery fire
with a suckling's persistence
assessing eyes gauge you
training flame to twin points,
sharp for no prizes hunted
with the clan that dreams by day
and is not satisfied, so also
from the twin lobes of day
a genie springs facing
two ways, you face which way?
Soon after, it quitted the road
and took into the woods, growing
every moment larger and stronger,
raising instead of dust the dry leaves
with which the ground was thick covered,
and making a great noise with them
and the branches, bending
some tall trees round in a circle
swiftly and very surprisingly,
though the progressive motion
of the whirl was not so swift
but that a man on foot
might have kept pace with it.

    Stone with chisels lifted
from working, steel
      ringing from stone!
Towers converse across

            the intervals,
ages of the ant rotate
            through each passing eye,
but friend, how stands the hour?
And where is my similar?

Heron leaving the pond
whitely sheeted, and banner
taken in from the staff
fly in the breast of one
lying in muddy green
with his gear slackened near him.
With the world, for the world,
trackless in exchanges
    not of the world.
Mild days invading winter,
warm days and mild low cloud
bathe the sleep of the hunter.
So his ribs sweeten
with the unseasonal clemencies
of a false August.
But he has lined out ahead,
not fallen back. His rust flowers
from the crowning treachery of worn gold.
Cities beneath cloud-surge
break into patchy view
through that domed breathing.
The ordeal from which he rests
has not yet concluded.
Do not touch him! but follow,
for he set out in this way
when the tribe mixed its ecstasies
and blundered through the circle.
In him the city lifts
a hillock of roofs, long falls
of vine greening an alley,
an unsuspected mountain
spiraling its spine
to the heart's blackened hidings
streaming in a mild rain:
follow saith its deep veil, here you shall
never be alone.

Parable with Broken Frame

An old architect at a littered worktable
  sits through morning, eyes fixed on ocean,
intent through evening at the study window,
  motionless though his hand rebuilds years.

Down razory defiles to the rockledge landing
  stands of flittergold awash in wind,
and through soft lolling labia of the waves
  tiny boats coming in, setting out.

Priest and corpsedresser begin the climb to his house,
  their empty craft nibbles at spindrift.
A bridegroom and his man steer for the islands,
  plinky music unrolls with their wake.

A last stone has been set in place, final tile,
  the bride folds her face in streaming hands,
the black duo mounts to the door and goes in.
  All of these I have been, none holds me.

Posthouse

Hearing gone rain plink into a cistern from the roofcorner,
amplified down a swift tunnel enlarging yet clarified –
long after a thatch-haired groom stabled and fed my horse
and I have climbed to my room and lie awake, not
exhausted from my mission this time, simply alert
as never quite before, with acuity not quite
personal for the night horizon through leafage,
rustling of the morning star that had been evening's star,
and the fading dialogue, dialectic, diaboli:
Now I know what my sins are. – You do not know what your sins are.
Plink of the remainder from what had dissolvingly
leaned across the province, slate gables, and the messenger
I then was, and had there opened a corridor
down which disinterestedly I might find passage.
And what I would have heard was the itineraries
of another man's travels, and that man was myself.

Seeing two or three lines of a parchment letter
slightly magnified, boundaries disengaging
furry luminous shadows from their support –
not the pauses of stagecraft, nor the gleams of spurious
admiration lifting them, but the planes
parallel and plural among them filling out,
with the nothing about which they can declare nothing
fountaining while they tremble into or past question.
All the while my veined hand pressed them in place
on veined oak planking, blood to sap humming like the sail
that tugged at rope in my grip as the chopped harbor
widened around the jetty's hook and tension
in the sheet slackened momentarily, then
firmed for the last stretch.
                              And what the ink disengaged
as a squiggle of known headland from scudding grey
was another man's unknown terms, and those were my own.

Sniffing dawn's hollyhocks as they brush the sill,
wet speartips dipping a little in cool drifts
from unseen brightenings that glint the grooved wood,
paint gulleying glacial cracks under the same wet.

The eye of the body is not always blind. Sniffing
the eyeless soul spurting in turns along stalks
I had not seen from the dusky door, had often
overlooked, but met now and greeted. Loosening
were a knot's interferences. I could say
that I stood at that window and saw rain in the wheelruts
both mud and silver, for that would have been the finding.
But I had found the flower. Straw-flecked courtyard set
on stacked settlements, stalks vaulting then withering along
uncoiling longitudes, turmoils of succession.
Fiber of mixed evils and boons a seed for the savior
who spilled along one jut as phallus and the other as god,
spores of good expanding incalculably if not nipped by
bunglings fouler than mire. And through me that rope, passing.

White Deer Running

Baucis and Philemon, having forgiven their killer Faust
and been resurrected to this life, to reenter their rest,
have come south and bought a stone house in the Morvan.
Undulating woodlots, hamlets beyond Autun.
Windows west only, into the long evenings
at midsummer, butterflies wavering in throngs
while rooms hold off heat with deep walls and embrasures.
Serendipity and sublimity are peasant sisters
waiting behind trees for farmers to find them, scuffle
with a pod of wild boar, and extend a barn from the wall.
Sublime and serendipitous, their last possession
for a renewed aging, lindens cooling each description.
The forest is named *Socrate*, a leader of the Resistance
dialectical in his disappearances,
and the barn wall was used for executions, by which side
there are varying reports. This too is to be had
in the idyll of ownership, a filmy disturbance
across the tabletop's oak grain, brown generations,
apples mounded in a plain crock, clear wines
draping colors over board and fruit, all this the senses
manufacturing from drift and ripple of syllables
before anything can be verified, yet the sheen falls
across an excellence of properties in trust
to no single appetite, in a place where sheen seems made fast.
   Narrow, the gate into our garden. A black sucking,
and waters crash, but you must not cry out or cling.
And then you are there, and you may come back if you choose
and report, though boasting is indecent, there are other ways.
Space there is not really different nor the sun,
but attachment is not what holds you, all that has gone.
         But that is
no possession: left listening and seeing, I was.
Apples, glass with ruddy window in its belly, the ruse
of solidity calling across the spoken was and is.
A low forest in Burgundy, woodlots in Massachusetts,
the last field before that drop where the river cuts.
   Against the clearing's edge
   at evening, already sliding
   among the indistinct

stems of December trees,
white deer running.
It was perhaps an hour
over the page, Arjuna's
refusal and the protracted
gleams of his charioteer.
When I looked out the window,
ranked birches turned in wind
silver through shadow, over
white deer standing.

Thonon-les-bains, Upper Terrace

With amnesiacs, she explained, her means was speech: to lever them
		back
by bending the throat's moan, suddenly memorious.

If a story may be halted while the life flows, it follows:
life is no story. Might we recall, then, what it is?

Below, a steamer preserved from the pre-First-War haven
nudged the landing's tongue. From its belly, a moist hoot.

A city gardener drenched rosebud clods with a hose.
To wait there above Leman halted by a layover
dearly companioned and, meeting this other, to let
afternoon's vast cup exhale vaporous fire
was to tap a vintage I had forgotten planting.

As a tyke in rubble streets, she had been dragged with sisters
by their starved mother in front of a tank. The precious *I*
is the pointedness of untold momenta. It stopped.

The cipher *God* was not so strange to the ancients, but then
the ancients had not become quite so strange to themselves.

Deft with camera, she squints and rewinds, that some of it
might be netted and hauled, and behind, gathered waters
stilled in their moving by the abyssal eye of good.

And if
		it is not a stretch of carpet thudded out on looms,
if it is not plotted, what is it like, then, existence?

(Unplotted answers will abandon aim, it seems,
without abandoning their course through awareness.)

143

Like a sound rising steadily through wearied alertness.
So do you choose to receive from that low hum of the chorus,
its unison at the frequency of an archer's breastbone,
or a keel pressing into the cold surge, riding level,
from it do you choose the arrow that shows two points
only so as to prong the eyes of evil, one unswerving thrust
carried by this sound that attains, that does not end,
subtlest of the creators? – But assent, like the air, already breathes.

In a Railway Compartment near Glarus

If it were solely three Croatian workers
talking of war in Croatia
who made me shut my eyes,
even to their city on the sea
Assisi-like, smoking,
where a stair tread
though grooved smooth leads to no exit;

if them alone, I wouldn't have shuddered
at the impulse to grow dark,
sporadic but twisting from the core,
then at its raw opposite,
Henry lunging down passageways
cursing his sons and Eleonore, Harry
craving some blessèd door, a young queen
hot between aging sheets, or a crack shearing
through the stone roof to grant him different issue
out over rivers, flocks, forests,
cunny's gate or bird's beak for blood's ire –

shivered at all of it and longed
to turn it into a turning, only thus
to see nothing though it all be there,
blink all gates blind though the wall rear up.

Then it came, swinging from the side, a tunnel.
Rumbling tons aimed us
with a steward two carriages ahead
tilting a tinkling tray of drinks
and bent flawlessly, entering –

and through that sleeving dark I groped
armless, like torsoes in the Book of the Dead
(twisting from the seed but not towards darkness),
for the skull's ridge, its pale fissure,
ladders rotted or thrown down,
beginning to remember the steadied river
overhead, radiantly fast.

Never You, in Those Ships, nor to Those Towers...

The means may seem to have slipped your grasp, distractingly splendid.
As if you came to Vézelay and heard behind doors
massed choirs already into their requiem. In dry grass
huddles clustered near an angle that released
a trickle of soprano, trombone, and contrapunto
while over the roof in deepening blue drifted Jupiter.
The gangway was being pulled up: such the illusion.
When singers left with families to cars down the long hill,
their vast plea finished, stragglers inside mooned at lit stone.

But what in you can awaken, to bear and not look away,
neither to cry for intervention nor to intervene,
may have no rendezvous on the choired ridges of July.
The ranged faces, cleared, recousined, may be no more your means
than a black lake you happen to come on at midsummer,
waves shoving inshore from the relentless passage
of boats in hundreds, running lights and mast lamps gliding
from some festival for the city, that means densely its own end,
engines humming, wealth pulsing one way down the dark.

Time is the boy downshore sorting gleams among pebbles,
and time is the girl sidling up wide steps to the narthex.
His eyes part the sheens of strata over endragoned nuclei,
hers penetrate pillared gate and avenue to the prepared
table of making and unmaking. And time marries time
though they will be separated, time and again, by the blade of fire
and our pity for their pain, sung in choruses, will have been misplaced.
What they met in each other was more than themselves, and it passed
through them to meet itself, so that lustres drenching the beach
withdrew with the wave, and footsteps trickled down stone.

And Fresh Cuttings from Like Things...

May it be that one morning given to me in this garden
the pack and walking stick, the boot with taped inner heel,
will carry foot only, bread and four-color map, and go with me
unburdened of agitation to the edge of Flussturheim.

There, not the copper beech surging from cobbles, that plume
burnishing the black root's force while thrusting sun away,
not that but its double will fill the air there, silver-pale, exhaling
the rustle of the latch in the door-catch to the beyond.

And I shall not startle, for near that trunk rises
the gurgle of the fountain of recollection, in Flussturheim.
Surge and relieving source. And I shall drink there before
coming to the low parapet belting town from river.

May it be that the haze will burn off, and the confluence
shine through beneath the notch, with its ford where
one king was slashed while crossing, and the murderer
became another king, but only the toppled man hero.

For it will be there, under potato gardens, tilted vines,
by the toll bridge open now to free passage, that heroes
will have set out for the crossing, leaving the moon foliage
of passion's copper, and entered into a plane of the far garden.

Below on the stone span, in blooded homespun, a girl
hooded alone at mid-arch, market basket on the rail
quite empty, her inscrutable gaze filling with the same green
that I might be conning and the identical hill line, but altered

by their having berthed long in her, refinding their way down
her stem of quiet, along meilinated quick to the remakings
within rootlets that surpass undoings and the suck downward,
force that rivers reversion but makes of return a tower.

She will not be waiting there for one of the heroes.
Nor will they pass there, processionally relinquished,
not in Flussturheim, where they have ridden out already
and left the years channeled and tapering towards rapids,

years that were, and that are, years in eye and in heart
going down – and she will close one over the other and go out
on a fire-cut path of seeing, as its live tendril, past moored
flat-bottoms square at prow and stern aslosh with gold-pale leaves,

and the azure-backed kingfisher bursting from shoreline shrubs,
along her own corridor, through the harshly oncoming, oh my girl.

Kirschdieb

Sooty rogue of the middle air
   shunning the curlew's bog
   and shag-delighting spume

came down on the cherry branch
that angled up to my window

and he asked, *Do you recognize me?*
   I answered, *I have hardly known myself.*
He asked, *And the wild Celtic Fathers?*
   I said, *You are not Him, but I hear the rills of home.*
He asked, *Has Merlin eluded?*
   I said, *The trunk still sways.*
Unblinking, he asked, *Will the eye see itself seeing?*
   I said, *Bending, the wing points,*
and then I asked, *What has shrouded my thought?*
   He said, *Love will tendril even through hell,*

then stripped every ripeness
   off the glistening knuckled twigs,
deleting what I was nurturing
   those summer days, whose evenings –
     but how did I see this
   unless through your climbing eyes –
   whose evenings ruddied the peaks.